JOANNE HORNIMAN has been a kitchenhand, waitress, editor, teacher and screen printer. She now writes full-time in a shed overlooking Hanging Rock Creek near Lismore, northern New South Wales. Her novels include *Mahalia*, *Little Wing* and *A Charm of Powerful Trouble*. *My Candlelight Novel*, told by Sophie O'Farrell, follows on from the story told by Sophie's sister Kate in *Secret Scribbled Notebooks*.

Praise for *Secret Scribbled Notebooks*:
'A deeply satisfying novel on every level.' *Viewpoint*

'The writing is beautiful … brightened by shafts of humour, romantic and introspective.' *Magpies*

'An evocative, dream-like read.' *Girlfriend*

MY
CANDLELIGHT
NOVEL

Joanne Horniman

ALLEN&UNWIN

Australian Government Australia Council for the Arts

This project has been assisted by the Australian Government through the Australia Council, its arts funding and advisory body.

First published in 2008

Allen & Unwin
83 Alexander Street
Crows Nest NSW 2065
Australia
Phone: (61 2) 8425 0100
Fax: (61 2) 9906 2218
Email: info@allenandunwin.com
Web: www.allenandunwin.com

National Library of Australia
Cataloguing-in-Publication entry:

Author: Horniman, Joanne

Title: My candlelight novel / Joanne Horniman.

ISBN: 9781741754858 (pbk.)

Dewey Number: A823.3

Cover design Bruno Herfst
Cover photograph by Getty Images/Marcus Lyon
Cover photograph by iStockphoto/Bill Noll
Text design by Sandra Nobes
Typeset in 10 pt ITC Galliard by Tou-Can Design
Printed in Australia by McPherson's Printing Group

10 9 8 7 6 5 4 3 2 1

'But mainly,
I'd like candlelight novel now.'

Jack Kerouac, in a letter to Allen Ginsberg,
20 June 1960

ACKNOWLEDGEMENTS

MY GRATEFUL THANKS go to the May Gibbs Children's Literature Trust for a residential fellowship in the Canberra studio where part of this book was written, and dreams dreamed during blissful naps on the blue sofa in the afternoon sunlight.

Also to the staff and students of Southern Cross University in Lismore, especially Dr Janie Conway-Heron, Senior Lecturer, Writing, in the School of Arts and Sciences, who generously allowed me to attend some of her lectures, and Dr Sacha Gibbons, whose tutorial I attended. Thanks to my friend Lainie Jones who facilitated it all.

Jacqueline Kent's colloquial translation of Rimbaud has finally been utilised, after many years. I'd also like to thank Kate O'Donnell, whose favourite writing advice from Jack Kerouac, 'Try never get drunk outside yr own house', inspired a portion of the dialogue.

PROLOGUE

ONE MORNING I WOKE and knew that I'd been talking in my sleep again.

I'd been dreaming of my mother of course – on my sleep-talking nights I always did. Kate tells me that my words were unintelligible, like a foreign language – but that was the way I had to speak to my mother, because what I wanted to say to her could not be said.

Hetty was sitting up in her cot, watching the pale light through the curtains on the French doors, and I lay there gazing at her for ages, loving every bit of her. I observed her tender neck and the roundness of the back of her dark head. And all my love for her distilled into the sight of that neck, so innocent, and the dark hair lying softly against it. How silent she was! Sometimes I thought that she'd never learn to speak, but spend her whole life mutely taking in the world, storing up her observations. When she saw I was awake, she grasped the bars of her cot and pulled herself to her feet, holding up one arm in a gesture of supplication. I took her into my arms; she smelt of talcum powder and urine, like an old woman. I fed her at once and changed her nappy and got her ready for a walk.

I pushed the pram along the path that ran parallel to the river, where overhanging fig trees made a dark tunnel through the mist. The riverbank was a wilderness of rainforest trees, black in the pre-dawn light. And as I trudged I recited poetry in my head; I often did this because walking and poetry had a rhythm that belonged together. My best trudging poem was 'A Prayer for My Daughter', by W. B. Yeats. It was a poem full of love and hope, for what else is there when you have a child?

The only sound was the rhythm of my feet and the wheels of the pram on the path, muffled by wet leaves. Moisture dripped from the trees. My hair must have been jewelled with tiny beads of it. When I put my hand to my head it came away wet.

In the gloom I half expected something magical to appear: a witch with a wart on her nose, Rumpelstiltskin, or for preference a dozen handsome brothers, one with a swan's wing instead of an arm. But it was just early-morning Lismore as usual. I came to the deserted court house, and the council car park, where I saw a man, his face tenderly blurred from lack of sleep, who looked as though he was wandering home from a drinking session.

When I got to the end of our road, instead of continuing down the main street, I turned right. There, a rattly bridge sprang across the river in a sort of leap of faith, from a shop called Planet Music to a hotel called the Winsome, which was a charming building of old, dark brick, with verandahs, overlooking the river.

On the bridge I paused to peer over the railing into the muddy water, and the dream I'd woken from came back to me. I'd been trying to write to my mother, but every attempt failed. I'd found myself writing on plastic (too shiny, and the ink wouldn't take), or on planks of fresh, smooth pine – but the words I attempted came out garbled, and then the ink faltered and gave out.

There was almost always a man pacing up and down on the bridge singing songs to the dawn, a sweet-faced man with curly grey hair, though he wasn't so old. He always smiled and waved to me and kept singing, and the homeless people who slept under the bridge yelled at him to shut up. I don't think he was a homeless person, just someone who had been unlucky in love, like me, and I felt the singing and pacing must help him.

I continued down Bridge Street, past the Winsome Hotel and various old shops and houses and the café where Kate used to work. As I passed the hotel, I always looked up at the side of the building where a white mixing bowl sat on a shelf inside the window of some scullery or kitchen. I loved the ordinary domesticity of it, the white bowl against the dark brick wall. My life at this time revolved around seeing each morning the stillness of the white bowl, and the singing man (or perhaps the still, pale face of the man as he paused to watch the sun rise in the sky; and the singing bowl in the window).

The place where I walked next was a run-down area that the local council had attempted to prettify, by plonking down a rusty old tractor in the middle of the roundabout. At that point I stopped to contemplate yet another old pub, a petrol station, a vegetarian café and a place that sold saddles. From there, the road went past wonky timber houses in the midst of paddocks, and my old school. There was a compound where the school kept farm animals, and I always took Hetty from her pram to pat the horse that hung its head hopefully over the fence, and to call to the cows and calves. They never responded, regarding us with deep suspicion. Then we moved on, over a small bridge that led to the other end of our street, and home.

None of this was ordinary or dull for either of us. I relished this morning ramble with my baby, crossing the river twice over different bridges, making a neat, circular walk, almost an odyssey.

Or it would have been an odyssey if the journey had been more adventurous and marked by many changes of fortune (though who is to say that each wandering walk was not a small adventure, that I did not come home each day a little changed by it?).

At the end of our journey, Samarkand squatted, inscrutable as always, overlooking the river.

The house is a crumbling two-storey weatherboard place on tall stumps; it's a guesthouse, of the cheapest and shabbiest kind. But there is something magical and other-worldly about it. Because it's on the river, in that place where earth and water meet, it sits on a threshold, a margin, a place of change. And it was in this muddy, watery place that I dreamed *I* might one day be transformed.

———

So this is my story. It will be about birth and death and love and sex, and I will tell it very quiet and slow, so if you want big bangs of action and excitement it's best you stop reading right now.

I will make it something after my own heart, tender and dark, a little candlelight novel, started this late summer night as my lover and baby daughter sleep in the big bed in the corner and my sister Kate leans thoughtful and sleepless against the railing of the dark verandah outside ... and I can tell already it won't even be a novel, but a tell-all memoir of my whole life so far ... but didn't Jack Kerouac write that we have got to *confess* our literature ...

part one

CHAPTER ONE

IN THE BEGINNING was my mother.

She was so young when I was born, still in her teens, and I know this not only from her age on my birth certificate, but from my memories of the way she *was*. Even before I was born I knew the sound of her voice, speaking *and* singing (and she sang often, in an ancient, eternal way, the way women since time immemorial must have sung on the edges of riverbanks at dusk). I knew all the ways she moved and walked and danced. I was her intimate, privy to every one of her moods. When I was born, she wailed like a banshee; her screams were horrendous. Well, childbirth *hurts*. I know that now.

The day I was born it rained, grey and soft and steady, with great streaks of water running down the windows like tears. Birth was my entry into what I consider heaven: the world, with all its weather, water, extraordinary skies, hallowed ground (for all of Earth is holy) and people, with their ambiguous, beating hearts.

When the midwife put me into my mother's arms, she said my name ('Sophie!') as though she'd always known me. We gazed at each other for a long time. I know it's customary for new mothers to have a thing about fingers and toes; first of all the big question of whether they are all there, and then the wonder that a fingernail could be so perfect and tiny (if only our mothers could look at our tiny, perfect hearts!). But my mother did none of that. She simply held me and looked into my face. 'Oh, she's beautiful!' she said.

I was born in my grandfather's house on the side of a wild mountain, and my early years on that wet, lush mountainside affected me for life. It's no wonder I have an affinity with water, and with overcast skies. I am at my best in a storm or a flood. I relish the run-down, the faded, the threadbare. I love twilight.

My mother sang to me and read to me before I could understand a word of any of it. I suckled with one hand tangled in her long hair and the other on her breast. Her body was the boundary of my world. I remember her so well: the smell of her and the coarse texture of her heavy black hair, and the way she walked with me on her hip, fearlessly striding through the world as if she owned it, trailing the hem of her long skirt through the dirt. I loved her so much.

She blew me streams of kisses when she went out, stepping into whichever burbling, asthmatic old car was fetching her away, her hem more often than not caught in the door and flapping farewell long after she turned her face away from me.

Sometimes she took me with her. I was there when Kate was conceived, waking one hot afternoon on the sticky back seat of a car to the sound of my mother engaged in something very urgent and pleasurable in the front. They were sitting upright, and I saw her face in profile, her mouth and eyes wide open, wearing an expression I couldn't recognise. Her cries subsided with a little sob, and I put my thumb in my mouth and stretched out one leg to push against the back of the seat, smiling because I knew she was happy. She turned around and looked at me as though she'd forgotten I was there, saying in wonder, 'Sophie

… are you awake?' She stretched out one arm to touch me. The man she was with, whom I would later come to call my father, shot me a look across the back of the seat and said, 'Hey, kid!'

And though I had no idea that such a thing as a sister even existed, somehow I knew that from now on I wouldn't be alone.

————

Whenever my mother went out and left me behind, my grandfather looked after me. I remember his face, grinning into mine. He was strong and wiry and brown and wrinkled. I remember his bare back, and the movement of his shoulders as he carried me around, my legs clasped around his neck.

Before I was two he'd already given me the names for things. Pawpaws, avocados, cherry tomatoes. Macadamia nuts! We foraged and ate these things in the wild of the garden, like savages. I sat astride his shoulders and said the words with bold gestures of my arms, commanding him to take me to them. 'Macadamia nuts!'

I sat on a low stool in his workshop, which was immense and rough-hewn. The sides were open to the view – and the weather – it was almost always raining. I watched him craft wood into sculptures. The smell of it! – his leather apron, streaked with dark sap, the hammering of his tools, the force, the rhythm, all this I remember.

The walls of his house were of stone and timber (both taken from the mountain we clung to; we were like mountain goats, living on a steep slope), and every wall was curved. Outside, waterspouts were shaped like dragons' heads. Stone faces bloomed amongst the ferns. Elaborately fashioned plant pots sprouted immense cacti. The winding paths were coloured lozenges of concrete – red, black, grey.

I remember an immense old chair; its graceful wooden legs had the air of belonging to an elegant animal – a greyhound

– so that sitting in it gave a feeling of borrowed power. My grandfather often cooked outdoors over an open fire. I feel sure I must have slept wrapped in animal skins in that place, though mostly we went around almost naked, it was so hot. The very air exuded moisture. Moving through it was like swimming.

He told me the tale of Jack and the beanstalk, and it seemed real and very possible, in that fairytale setting. Climbing any one of the plants in my grandfather's garden might lead you to the giant's castle, and the hen that laid the golden egg. I found a nest made in the ferns by our black hen, and a perfect, smooth brown egg. In that magical place, I crouched on the ground and tapped the egg carefully on a rock. It was golden inside, and I tipped it into my mouth and swallowed it.

I ate the Golden Egg!

But my mother took me away from all that.

Once upon a time I lived with my mother in paradise and I lost it all.

————

When my sister Kate was born at last, and grown to almost three years old, she and I were abandoned. First our mother went away (or so Michael O'Farrell told us), and then he abandoned us too.

If it hadn't been for Kate, who was sweet and compliant and eager for love, I am sure Lil would not have kept us with her. I was too savage and unruly and strange for anyone but my mother to properly love.

The day Michael O'Farrell left, it was clear to me that he wasn't coming back, and I was pleased. Before bed, Lil removed our filthy clothes and popped us into the bath. And it was while she was washing my mop of hair she discovered something tangled in its bush. She fetched scissors to cut it free, but I bit her, I so fiercely wanted to keep it. She only said sternly, 'That's enough, madam!' And at last produced the tiny doll I'd put in my hair for safekeeping, a plump naked infant with drawn-up legs and dimpled outstretched hands, its tiny hands and feet still bound with ropes of my black hair.

'What else are you keeping on your person, then?' she said, never guessing that I sometimes hid a small white pebble in my fanny. My body was the best hiding place for anything I wanted to keep safe.

If only I hadn't been torn from my mother. I ought never to have taken my fingers from her hair as I lay in her arms. That way, wherever she had gone, she'd have had to take me with her.

———

Lil lived in a house called Samarkand, which was like a house of dreams, with many rooms and meanings and odd encounters. The first morning, Lil took us into the faded old kitchen for breakfast, but before she could begin cooking, I took an egg, cracked it, and tipped it into my mouth (still searching for that magic, golden egg).

Without even letting on that she'd noticed what I'd done, Lil poached some eggs and slid them onto hot buttered toast with a sprinkle of parsley. And Kate and I sat up at the kitchen table and ate our eggs neatly as though we had been born to this life. (Kate: her pale, china-doll face small and solemn, her fine red hair that never seemed to grow lying flat and obedient to her scalp. Me: my bottom lip jutting out with defiance, my eyes challenging, hair to my waist as black as sin and as complicated.)

'There,' said Lil. 'Doesn't an egg taste better cooked than raw?'

(It did, but felt not nearly as magical.)

That night, when Lil went to kiss us goodnight, Kate held up her face eagerly, her lips ready, but I turned to face the wall. If I couldn't have my mother, I'd have nobody.

Lil never stopped offering.

I remember the night I gave in. I snatched her kiss and then turned away in shame. The need for love is like that for food. If you're hungry and it's offered to you, why not simply reach out and take it?

You can take, but you can choose not to give back. For a long time I took and took Lil's kisses like a starving person, but my heart had been pledged to my mother.

Chapter Two

As usual after my morning walk, I climbed the steps of Samarkand with Hetty on my hip and went to the kitchen to start the breakfasts. There were only two guests that day. They sat at separate tables, the man reading the morning newspaper, and the woman looking out the window of the breakfast room towards the river, her hand held up beside her mouth as though she had seen the unspeakable.

The man had almost no hair and a bulbous nose textured like a cauliflower. The woman had a squint, and deep lines running from the edge of her nose to the corners of her mouth, giving her an air of severe disappointment. Both of them had a physiognomy that told of another place and century – Victorian England perhaps; or a place where everyone was wounded or scarred in some way.

I served them and went back to the kitchen to feed Hetty her egg, feeling ineffably sad for people. How lonely, how flawed, how doomed everyone was. I thought how Hetty, in all her fresh perfection, would some day bear sorrow of some kind, while I, who am scarred inside where you cannot see, look ripe and ready for plucking.

I sat a plate onto the tray of Hetty's chair, and spooned egg into her little bird mouth (how willingly and trustingly she opened it for me!). A fresh surge of love for her overcame me. Her plump hands, the rings of fat round her neck, the way she flexed her toes as she ate!

'You're nice. You're *very* nice, did you know that?' I told her, firmly. Hetty put her head on one side, and smiled.

I thought about the poetry of kitchens. There seemed to be very little of it written, but there was so much to be captured, and a kitchen is the heart of the house, a place of pleasure and work. Not all of it is beautiful, but why should poetry only speak of beauty?

There's the begrimed stove-top, the splatters that tell of the pleasures of eating and the accompanying dreariness of cleaning up. I would like to see a poem on the not-so-secret squalor of under-the-sink, a poem about the moist shimmer of fat that accumulates under the griller after lamb chops have been cooked, and the astonished twinkle of a clean stainless steel sink. I love the smooth, cool body of the refrigerator against which I lay my cheek in hot weather, and the dance of the trembling, collapsible ironing board, the toasty smell of its warm cover. There are the worn rungs of chair legs, paint rubbed away by restless feet. If you're after beauty, there is the amber stream of hot tea coming from the pot.

And there, up in the corner of the coloured glass window, a little spider sits protecting her egg sac, the most hidden and domestic scene of all.

'Kitchen is a *green* word,' I told Hetty that morning. Kitchens always remind me of green, perhaps because these walls are green. And I love the word *kitchen*. Sometimes I think it's my favourite word. *'Kitchen, kitchen, kitchen.'*

Hetty blew egg at me and smiled. See how already my baby loved words, even though she couldn't speak them yet?

———

After we'd eaten our breakfast, I took her to Lil's room. Pulling back the curtains from the window, I pictured myself as some nineteenth-century housemaid rousing her mistress. Light flooded in, and I could see that Lil was already awake. She had been lying there in the darkened room, not moving. She shielded her eyes and exclaimed, 'The light! Oh, the light!' And for kindness I frisked the curtains back over the window a little.

Kate had gone away to university at the beginning of the year, and since then Lil had taken to lying-in in the mornings and leaving the breakfasts to me. At various moments of the day she was prone to wondering what 'my Katie' was doing now, and I had taken to doing the same. (*It's nine a.m. Wednesday. Kate, who has stayed up almost all night writing an essay on the Romantic poets, stumbles out to the shared kitchen to find that one of the people who also have a room in the house has breakfasted on squid. Again. She throws open the window to let in fresh – or other-than-squid – air and stands for a moment contemplating a back lane filled with garbage and stray cats.*)

Perching on the sill with Hetty on my knee, I peered between the curtains to the laneway that ran beside our house. (*We are two sisters, seven hundred kilometres apart, both currently contemplating insalubrious laneways.*) It had started to rain, and there was a dog in the Lismore lane, sniffing round the wooden stumps of the house over the way. The road was primitive, just a walkway really, made of earth. Because it seemed to be always raining, it almost never dried out, and it was this smell of damp that pervaded our house. Mould grew on almost every surface. I fully expected that ferns would sprout from the cornices one day.

I plonked Hetty down on the bed next to Lil, and went out for the breakfast tray, which I made room for on the bedside table.

Lil blew on her tea to cool it. She leaned forward and pursed her mouth to take a sip. I was reminded of the way Hetty ate, leaning forward in her high chair and taking food from the spoon with such a pretty scoop of her lips. Perhaps as people got older they really did revert to babyhood. Lil and Hetty seemed to have such affinity.

Now Lil was handing her a triangle of toast. Hetty, full to the brim with scrambled egg, couldn't possibly be hungry. She took the toast and pressed it between the palms of her hands, squeezing out the butter like water from a sponge. She let the toast fall onto the bed and leaned forward to touch Lil on the face.

'Sophie darlin', do you have a cloth?' (Do you see how readily endearments sprang from Lil's mouth?)

I lunged forward to wipe butter from my baby's hands with a teatowel, splaying her fingers and cleaning her creased little palms. While I was there I dabbed the butter from Lil's cheek. Lil and I never had proper conversations. We always spoke the comforting language of the everyday, and rarely revealed our more intimate thoughts. Today, Lil was engrossed in fussing about with Hetty.

Still feeling like a parlourmaid, I took the time to put a bit of spit and polish on the framed photographs that stood on the dressing table. There was a picture of Kate and me together when we were very young, not long after we'd come to Samarkand, looking, as Lil would have said, 'as though nobody owned us'. There was one of Hetty and me when she was a tiny baby. I was very puffy and pale; Hetty was wrinkled and pinkish. If we looked rather blurred and indistinct, it wasn't because of the poorness of the photography, it was because we were both still in the process of becoming. Shortly after that picture was taken we'd both unfolded into being mother and child, and I am pleased to say that these roles became us.

As a reminder of Kate's growing up and away, there was a picture of her with her friend Marjorie at their Year 12 formal, at the end of the previous year. Marjorie, as always, looked like a latter-day Snow White in a perfect little 1950s style frock, while Kate wore an old suit (!) that she'd found in Lil's cupboard. I'd advised her against it at the time, but had to admit now that she looked quite fetching and not at all masculine in it, her long red hair cascading over her shoulders.

The suit had belonged to Alan, Lil's son who had died, and it was his photograph that I did last (he had long hair in this picture, and wore some sort of ethnic shirt), spitting on the hem of my dress again and wiping the glass most tenderly. I had asked Lil once what he'd been like, and she'd said that he'd been a lovely boy, a beautiful, tender young man. 'But close,' she added. 'I mean, there was lots he didn't tell me. He often kept his feelings to himself. He was like you in that way.' And it pleased me to be thought to be 'like someone', even someone I wasn't related to, because it made me feel connected, the way other people were.

Lil finished what she wanted of breakfast, and had eaten very little. Passing Hetty to me, she clambered out of bed and went to her wardrobe to choose a dress. Great black moths spilled from the cupboard and flapped about the room as she rummaged around. They were not clothes moths, but must have loved dark spaces. I sometimes found them inside the fireplaces, where they drifted in clusters like giant flakes of ash.

Lil put on a red dress that morning (the colour of bravery, and love), and made up her face. She painted on a thick layer of powder and red lipstick that bled into the wrinkles radiating out from her mouth. Dressed, and made up, Lil made her way stiffly to the door with a proud expression on her face.

She sailed out into Samarkand, into her day.

CHAPTER THREE

I AM A READING girl, with a pale face, and glasses. People who become enthralled by the world of books, as I am, are often thought to have dull lives, but I feel that my own life is made of the stuff of myth. Or anyway, I intend to make it so.

Some say that books are an escape from *real life*. But the beauty of books is that they are crammed with real life. No one is more aware of *real life*, in all its trivia and glory, than a novelist. In novels you will find mention of things like measles, chocolate, ferry crossings (and eating chocolate on ferry crossings), train journeys, adultery (and adultery on train journeys), bacon, junkies, the Sydney Harbour Bridge, gas ovens, lost jewellery, wedding dresses, shower caps, snot, randy bakers, honey, miso soup, spider webs, lost mothers, abandoned children, rainforests, immortality, angels and toe rot.

Not to mention love. Novels are full of life's impurities, and love must be the most impure thing of all.

But now, with Hetty growing older, I couldn't read as much as I'd have liked. It's very easy to spend almost all day reading with a small baby at your breast, but now she needed to be talked to, and played with, and be read aloud to something other than the Great Works of literature. She had progressed from the plays of Oscar Wilde to board books full of pictures of ducklings and butterflies.

I made a habit of carrying her around the house and naming things for her. 'This is a wooden spoon, Hetty,' I would tell her, holding it aloft as I helped Lil make a cake. That day, I had occasion to point out the washing machine, the vacuum cleaner and the kitchen sink. I hid behind the sheets on the line and popped my head out at her, which made her laugh immoderately.

I took her across the road to the river, and showed her Kate's fig tree, a special, almost sacred place, since it was where Kate had dreamed her childhood away. Magpies, empty chip packets, and the greyhound racing track across the river completed Hetty's education that day, and afterwards we were both so worn out we went to our room for a nap.

————

That afternoon, while I was on my way to the kitchen, the phone in the hall rang. I lifted the receiver and heard the familiar chimes of the HomeLink signal.

'Lil?' Kate's voice was so small it was almost inaudible.

'No. It's me. How are you?'

There was a long, shuddering intake of breath. 'I'm lonely.' She drew the word out so that it was a wail of self-pity. *Looooooooonely.*

(O Kate!)

There was a sniffle on the other end.

'Where are you?'

'In a phone box on King Street.'

I put Hetty down onto the floor, where she crept over to the corner of the dim hallway and found something that interested her, I couldn't see what.

Leaning up against the wall, I pulled down a strip of photos from where I'd wedged them behind the pegboard over the phone table. Kate had recently had them taken in a photo booth. She had cut her long hair very short; she'd done it herself to save money and it was a bit ragged, but it suited her. I studied the progression the photos took, from the first caught-unawares shot, to carefully wary-looking, to increasingly confident to extravagantly posed.

'Stop crying, you eejit. Now. Describe for me exactly what you can see right at this moment.'

'O *God*, Sophie!'

'What? So you can see God, can you?'

'Noo-ooo! Okay... I see an ugly little tan-and-white terrier tied up to a post.'

'Why is it ugly?'

'Eyes too close together. Horrible gingery colour. Um... I can see a boy with a ring through his eyebrow. He looks really happy about something. Now the woman who must own the dog has just untied it... she's wearing a coat like a hessian sack, and her hair is all sticking up at the back of her head as though she's slept on it but I think she might have paid a lot of money to get it looking as terrible as that. Is that enough? I think I'm okay now...'

But she wasn't.

'O Sophie ... It's just that I don't know anyone. No one I can really talk to. And I was so sure when I came down here I'd make heaps of friends and all sorts of exciting things would happen. And with Alex still away in Europe ... I really thought he'd be coming back, you know? Marjorie's in Brisbane ... there's no you and Hetty and Lil ...

'And Sophie ... there's just something about the long shadows on a winter afternoon, and the light in my room, so tobacco-brown and gloomy, and...

'How's Hetty?' she finished up in a feeble voice.

'She's fine. Currently about to put a dead cockroach she just found on the floor into her mouth.'

Lil appeared in the doorway that led from the kitchen into the hallway. 'Is that my Katie?' she said. She picked Hetty up, took the cockroach from her with distaste, and threw it away. Handing Hetty over to me, she took the receiver.

I left her to talk, and went to Kate's room. It was exactly as she had left it earlier in the year.

Soon after she'd started university Kate had written:

Dear Sophie,

At last, my life is like a book!

I'm sitting at my table on a Friday night and my teeth are aching with excitement. I've lit a candle in honour of writing to you, and when I've finished I will blow it out. (If Lil is reading this she should be assured that I'm also writing with the aid of electric light and am not ruining my eyes: the candle is there to gaze at and to steady my focus on you, my dear reader.)

Outside lies King Street, Newtown. I cannot sleep for lights flashing through the window (nor do I want to). Living here is like fronting a different kind of river than the one that flows past Samarkand: tonight this river is in flood, with people and traffic going past. There are short, sharp bursts of voices and vehicles above the steady background hum.

Earlier, I went out and joined the throng; most people were with groups of friends, but there were many solitary people like myself. I bought a takeaway kebab and came back here and sat on the windowsill to eat it, looking down into the street.

But already I know the bed, my piles of books, the one cupboard I have for clothes, all too well. The problem is that nothing here will move position unless I move it. I miss coming into my room and knowing that you've been there, by a dent in the quilt not made by me, a black hair left on the pillow, mandarin peel scattered over the desk, or the fact that one of my books has disappeared, perhaps forever.

Whenever I come back to my room here I want to shout, 'Hello-o-o? Is there anyone home?' I would have to answer myself, whispering a small, meek 'Yes'.

I don't know what university will be like yet, as I've only had one week of lectures. I know no one, of course, and most of the other students seem to know each other from high school, and they mostly live at home, so they disappear at the end of the day.

On our reading list is Ulysses. *I've bought a second-hand copy that is at least four hundred years old, a big old doorstopper of a book, disintegrating and well-thumbed. The cover is black, with only the words* Ulysses *and* James Joyce *in large white letters on it.*

And the cover has been stuck back on with masking tape, and inside there are already notes from previous students. I've dipped into it, and some of it is wonderful. The bit I like best so far is the one that begins, Mr Leopold Bloom ate with relish the inner organs of beasts and fowls.

It describes him going out and buying a kidney for breakfast, cooking and burning it, and throwing the burnt bit to the cat. He takes his frowzy wife Molly a cup of tea, and goes and sits on the toilet reading the paper. (By the way, do you know that Irish cats say Mrkrgnao?)

Some of the book is almost unreadable, and some totally unreadable. At one of those parts a previous student has written in the margin: Why did I do this course? *I well may feel the same by the end, but for now, Sophie, it is sublime! And actually, the unreadable bits somehow make it even better, because life is mysterious and never completely knowable, don't you think?*

My teeth seem to be back to normal now, so I think I'll try to get some sleep. So I'll blow out the candle and say goodnight.

My best and most fervent love to Hetty and Lil,
Your sister Kate

I picked up one of Kate's books (*Nausea*, by Jean-Paul Sartre) and took it to the bed and lay down with Hetty. Kate had written with such excitement about her new life, and now she was lonely. I had not written back to her. I am too lazy. Besides, she knows I seldom confide in her, but she is such an innocent, and insists on pouring out her heart anyway.

Opening the book, I found a long strand of her hair that she had left between the pages.

A relic.

Kate was in the habit of absently taking one of her own hairs and marking her place with it. This hair was like a filament of copper wire, but finer. It caught the light and flashed out the colours red, gold, mauve, and even green (yes!). My sister has extraordinary hair.

I remember how I once unexpectedly found one of my own hairs caught between the pages of a book, the shock of recognising it as mine. It was long, coarse and black, the dull black of wood stoves or pieces of ash.

Now, finding Kate's hair was like finding a part of myself. My sister Kate: who as a child had a tiny, pale, porcelain solemn face and thin red hair lying flat to her scalp. Who now lived in a room above a greengrocer in the inner Sydney suburb of Newtown. She shared a kitchen and bath, and the other residents left squid hanging out of bowls in the refrigerator. Even the forlorn appearance of the little legs dangling over the side of the bowl was enough to make Kate melancholy.

She lived uneventfully, going to university and then home again. She longed to meet someone she felt an affinity with... There was Alex of course, a boy from Sydney whom she'd met here in Lismore last year, but he had gone to Europe and had not yet come back. He wrote to her, which left her with feelings of lingering hope...

She lived on sardines and tinned tomatoes and longed for Turkish delight. She missed us and she was lonely...

———

As I was lonely. And that was the truth, it really was. Even though I said I relished our walks (and I did!), when I got up early every morning and strapped Hetty into her pram and walked her across the river and then home again, I was lonely, lonely.

Not lonely for Hetty's father Marcus, not anymore, or even always especially for Kate – it was a loneliness of the light perhaps, as Kate said, or a loneliness of the world being so large and we just small people in it. Lonely, lonely, said the wheels of the pram under the silent misty early morning figs, lonely on the concrete path, lonely on the soft fallen leaves. The man who sang on the bridge at dawn knew lonely, so did the people who slept under it. All of us know what lonely is, and we accustom ourselves to it, but that does not stop the loneliness of the light and the world and all the people in it.

But in truth I walked not always unaccompanied. Sometimes Oscar Wilde (Oscar Fingal O'Flahertie Wills Wilde) walked beside me, silent companion of the soul. I felt such an affinity with this witty and outrageous Irish playwright. If he was still alive, he would be more than one hundred and fifty years old, though he didn't even live to be fifty. He said once, 'I have never learned anything except from people younger than myself', so I like to think he enjoyed my company. I always imagined him in a beautifully tailored long black coat with an astrakhan collar (astrakhan: horrible concept, made of the skin of young lambs – or worse, even *unborn* lambs – with wool like fur). But I'm working from wild surmise, as I don't truly know whether he wore astrakhan or not.

And as we walked, Oscar strewed flowers about him, gladioli and lilies.

And did the people of Lismore catch them and take them home?

Well, some thrust them aside angrily; some trod them underfoot, not seeing them (or indeed him, or even me and Hetty for that matter). But others caught them gladly and took them back to their manky kitchens and displayed them in old juice bottles, or in 1930s vases of indescribable ugliness inherited from their maiden great-aunts.

———

I had spent the autumn and part of that winter reading the works of the Brontës. Emily may have given us the archetypal soul mates in Catherine and Heathcliff, but Charlotte is my favourite. The life of feeling and passion was everything to her. She gave her heroines what she could never have in real life, and the undertones are so lustful I believe her books must be the sexiest ever written. I first read *Jane Eyre* at fourteen; that book is so depraved that it ought to be kept out of the way of impressionable young girls.

Hetty learnt to crawl while Lucy Snowe waited for her Professor in *Villette*. She tore the cover from *Jane Eyre* while I was reading *Wuthering Heights*. She chewed the spine of *Shirley* and smeared butter and Vegemite over the portrait of Charlotte

Brontë on the inside cover. Despite her propensity to destruction, and her frequent tears and grizzles, Hetty was a happy baby, and I think that is the most that one can hope for in babies, that pure and unself-conscious happiness which must surely be our natural state.

And while it seemed to me sometimes that I had a meagre life, and the often meagre lives of the women in the Brontë books shaded into and coloured my own, the richness did as well, the glory of being alive. I would get up at night and wander the house in my threadbare chenille dressing-gown the colour of old roses (and sometimes, it seemed, the scent of them as well), then go to the kitchen and sit and stare, my hands cupped around a bowl of hot chocolate (which somehow tastes best in bowls). Or I'd lie on my side with a book open next to me, and Hetty asleep in her cot nearby, while the wind wuthered around the house. And at those times I'd think how lucky I was, really. I had books and a baby and a room of my own and what else does a girl need?

Chapter Four

To immediately answer my own question, a girl needs quite a lot, really.

A day or two after Kate's call, sick of doing nothing but reading and housework, I packed a bag with all the things Hetty might conceivably need, and prepared to go to the university. I had enrolled because I needed a qualification if I was going to be eventually able to support us both. I'd only decided on enrolling a little while ago, so I couldn't start until mid-year. But I wanted to go and get the feel of it all, and imagine myself there for the next few years of my life.

That day, I also squeezed into the already bulging bag things that *I* might conceivably need: a brand-spanking-new copy of *Madame Bovary*, an apple, and a bar of chocolate. Slinging the bag over the back of the pram, I pushed it to the bus stop. It was an unromantic Monday morning, one of those days when I noticed tiresome things like the scruffiness of people's sneakers and the way apple labels and chewing gum had been stuck onto the benches. While I waited for the bus I thought about the poetry of bus trips. Where, I wondered, was the poetry about young women with babies who must struggle onto buses (the hands-full juggle for the fare, the fold-up pram hooked over the arm, the baby spinning a web of drool over the mother's shoulder, the lurching progress up the aisle to fall down into a juddering seat, the other passengers staring at you as if this was *just what you deserved*).

The bus wound away from the shops and through suburban Lismore. I held Hetty on my lap and we both looked out the window, swaying gently with the movement of the vehicle. I thought how dull it all was: the fast-food places clustered on Ballina Road, the timber cottages set in inevitable gardens, and yet inside me there was a spark of anticipation. At the university the bus spat us out onto the footpath. Its doors sighed loudly as they shut, and it roared away, as though pleased to be rid of us.

The university looked like a fortress. The entrance had a boom gate and sentry box. I saw young people in cars trying to bluff their way in, attempting to drive closer to the top of the hill, but they were banished to the student car park at the bottom. Being on foot with a pram I was able to whisk past the grey-uniformed men unnoticed.

Buildings straggled up the hill, connected by winding paths. At the foot stood the Union building, and a plaza where people sat eating and drinking in the sun. Beyond that, I found a building that said *School of Contemporary Music*. Because Hetty's father Marcus was a musician, I've always exposed her to music in case she turns out to have an aptitude for it.

So I went in. There were sounds that you might have called music coming from various rooms, most of it hesitant or discordant, starting and then stopping. I went down corridors where people stood in little knots talking to each other, people with dreadlocks and glamorous ragged clothing that exposed glimpses of beautiful flesh. I felt like such an outsider. Everyone around me was purposeful; they knew what they were doing; they belonged. No one else toted a baby; no one else wore a pilled cardigan over a dress that had seen far better days (though in truth, I dressed that way deliberately to show that I was above such considerations as appearance).

I stopped to read the notices posted on the walls; most were lists of class groups. I read some of the names, trying to get a sense of the real people they must belong to. That boy over there in the long black tailcoat over torn jeans and bare feet – surely he couldn't have one of these ordinary names – such as the Michael Hart who did drums on Tuesdays at one p.m.? I saw a beautiful girl greet him warmly; as I watched them hug (it took a long, long time and involved much caressing of her smooth bare back) I felt a pang of sorrow. No one here knew me, nor would I ever be greeted in such a way.

I slunk away, feeling even more of an alien and an outsider. I pushed Hetty up the hill till I reached the building that said *School of Arts and Humanities*, which was where I had enrolled. The people there appeared to be even busier and more purposeful than the music students. I looked down at Hetty, who lolled back in her pram with her big toe in her mouth. She looked so delightfully unimpressed by her surroundings that I immediately picked her up and kissed her.

I found the library, bought a cup of tea from the cart outside, and sat in the sun with Hetty at my breast. Self-consciously, I took *Madame Bovary* from my bag and read, aware that no self-respecting university student would be caught dead with such a book. I had only just begun reading it, and at that stage thought that it was entirely delicious. I loved the bit where Emma Bovary licked the last drops of wine from the bottom of a glass with her tongue.

I finished my tea and, leaving the pram at the entrance, carried Hetty into the library. It was modern and airy and light; a stairwell in front of windows two storeys high had rainforest plants growing in it. A set of carpeted metal steps led to the upper floor. They were long, with gaps between the treads, the sort of stairs I knew I had to protect Hetty from falling down.

I made my way up those alarming stairs to the literature section, plopped Hetty onto the floor and started to browse. I soon had my arms filled with books – I was lost in a happiness of books – but when I thought to look at Hetty again she had disappeared.

The books fell from my arms, but I scarcely noticed. And the library became a place of danger.

The rows of shelves were ill-lit tunnels; I ran past them, scanning to left and right along the ranked metal shelving. The heavy door that led to the fire escape banged shut with a hollow, threatening echo. The doors of the lift made a noise like a sword cutting the air. I bumped into a man. His face loomed over my shoulder as I looked back without apology; the eyes bulged in his pale face.

I was sweating, but my legs and arms were chill. I think I forgot to breathe. My heart thrashed, but I willed my mind to stay clear. It was possible that someone might have found her, or worse, taken her. I would go to the front desk and ask them to keep a lookout for anyone leaving with her. I would demand a search party!

Then I remembered the airy, dangerous stairs I had come up, and I ran for them.

They came in view just as Hetty arrived at the top. She had an odd way of crawling – instead of going on her hands and knees she sat, and scooted along on her bottom, and had become incredibly fast.

I called to her, but she didn't seem to hear. She sat there, her neck as tender as a mushroom stalk, looking down the long drop as if considering what to do next. She made to move forward, but before I could get to her, a girl came leaping up the stairs two at a time and scooped her into her arms.

'Is she yours?'

'Yes,' I said. 'Thank you. Oh thank you, thank you.'

'It was nothing,' said the girl, smiling at Hetty and squeezing her on the foot before walking away with the sort of loose, insouciant stroll that should be set to music. With my heart singing (my baby was safe!) I went back and picked up the books I'd dropped all over the floor. Hetty belatedly decided to burst into tears; her hands probed into my dress for the comfort of a breast, so I sat on the floor between the shelves and fed her. Then I took my books down to the front desk.

'Do you have a card?' asked the librarian.

I took my card from the city library out of my purse, knowing as I did so that it wouldn't be sufficient.

The girl at the desk had a pretty face and short brown hair so straight and beautifully cut that a poet could have written several sonnets to it. But when she saw the card I presented she looked as though she'd sucked a lemon. I thought it a waste that someone so pretty should feel so sour. She looked at my inferior library card as though she wanted to incinerate it with her breath. 'It is forbidden to use this library without proper authorisation.'

I so wanted those books. There was one about the life of John Keats the poet, very promisingly thick, and so pristine I could tell that no one ever bothered to take it out.

'I'll be a student here very soon,' I said, but she shook her head and dismissed me.

I thought that I should dump the books somewhere and slink away with my tail between my legs, but the girl who'd rescued Hetty, who'd been standing in the queue and must have seen it all, said quietly, as I passed her, 'I'll get them out for you, if you like.'

I waited for her outside the library. In a while she came out and placed the books ceremoniously into my arms. 'It is forbidden,' she intoned, and we laughed. I noticed that she herself had only borrowed a pile of CDs. 'You have exactly two weeks,' she told me. 'Don't get them back late – it's a dollar a day per item.'

I thought how trusting she was. She didn't even know me. And though I love them, I am notoriously bad with books – I lose them, I give them away, they fall apart willy-nilly under my fingers. I allow Hetty to eat them.

'My name's Sophie O'Farrell,' I told her, in case she should need to chase the books up. 'And I live in a boarding house called Samarkand – you know that big old house down near the river?'

She nodded.

She had long, dark, perfectly flat hair tucked behind ears that were small and delicate and had almost no lobes. She dressed like a certain kind of boy, in plain jeans and T-shirt, and along with the CDs she carried a slim case that might have contained some tool or other.

'And my baby's called Hetty.'

'Hetty,' repeated the girl with a smile. Ever alert to her name, Hetty looked up and took her fingers out of her nose.

'And I'm Becky Sharp,' said the girl, holding out her hand.

'Really!' I exclaimed. We stopped, and I took the hand, which was long and slender, and very cool.

'What is it about my name? You're not the first person who seems to think it's remarkable.'

'Becky Sharp's the heroine of a famous nineteenth-century novel,' I said, 'called *Vanity Fair*. And she was the author of her own life, a wonderful thing to be, don't you think? She made sure it was an audacious and adventurous life, too. Full of surprises.'

I could also have added that her namesake was beautifully manipulative and self-serving. She had to be, as she was an orphan, like me, and had no mama to arrange a marriage for her. She had to fend for herself.

'I like the sound of her,' said Becky Sharp. 'But I don't read novels. I play the flute.'

I wanted to point out that surely these two things weren't mutually exclusive, but she had been kind to me. We'd been walking down the hill all this time, and when we got to the car park at the bottom she said, 'D'you need a lift?'

Becky Sharp's car was low-slung and old and iridescent green; it looked like an enormous frog. It was an old Citroën, she said, a CX. She stowed the pram in the back and opened the passenger door for me. Then she went around and folded herself into the driver's side. Becky Sharp's arms and legs were so soft and pliable they seemed almost boneless. And every part of her matched. With limbs like that, it was fitting that she had those adorable little lobeless ears and a tiny rounded nose so flat she looked almost like a painting by Modigliani. And her eyes were slightly slanted, and her mouth a veritable rosebud, with a protruding lower lip. I wanted to reach out and touch her.

She saw me watching her and smiled. Turning on the ignition, she pressed a lever, and the car lifted itself up like an animal about to pounce. 'Pneumatic suspension,' she explained.

As the green car slid out of the university car park, I felt a great sense of triumph. I had penetrated the fortress of the university and had come away in style, with an armful of forbidden library books and a girl named Becky Sharp.

The ride was very companionable. She put on a CD of Beth Orton (I gave her top marks for good taste in girl singers) and I retrieved the chocolate from my bag and gave her half. We laughed a lot, though I can't remember quite what we said, and arrived at Samarkand far too soon.

Gliding home in that car with its all-out, old-fashioned shabby elegance would stay with me for a long time. And the way Becky Sharp left her green frog car purring in front of Samarkand and ran slender-hipped up the stairs with Hetty's pram and down again to drive off with a wave of her hand, that stayed with me too.

CHAPTER FIVE

AFTER PERSISTING ALMOST to the end of the book, I found that I *hated Madame Bovary*! Oh, some of the words were captivating, but who was she? this young wife of a country doctor living in a place called Yonville (Yawnville). She was a wraith, an absence, a giant hole in the middle of a lot of wonderful description. I thought that this *Flaubert* (you pronounce it Flo Bear, which always puts me in mind of a bear in a mob cap and apron in a children's book), this Flo Bear might have thought the world beautiful but he didn't much care for the people in it. Everyone in the book was awful, and I thought he did Emma Bovary an injustice in portraying her as so... *wet*! It was one of the few books I have been unable to finish. It made me want to chew on my wrists in frustration. It curdled my milk and gave Hetty indigestion, and I flung it across the room and paced the verandah with my hair and eyes wild. Because I knew what happened in the end (she dies, she dies, she dies – which seems the fate of every fictional adulteress), and I couldn't bear the tedium of getting to it.

————

I was sick of being spinsterish and bookish and alone. And all that wanting and wanting and not-getting that women since time immemorial have accepted as their lot – it was a bore in real life.

———

So I whiled away my time, waiting to go to university. I often didn't bother getting dressed, and lay on my bed reading, my dressing-gown tied with an old silk scarf of Lil's. In this garb I would venture out to change the sheets on the guests' beds, heaping them on the floor outside the bedrooms, and then forgetting all about them in the imperative of feeding or changing Hetty. I baked chocolate cake and ate it with peppermint tea on the back steps late at night while Hetty slept. I piled my hair up on top of my head and used chopsticks to pin it, then took it down again and let it flow over my shoulders. I dyed one of my nursing bras purple; the effect was so frightful that I had to go to the bridge and toss it into the river at the first opportunity. I washed the dinner dishes late at night whilst listening to music turned up LOUD (*viva* Patti Smith!) until some guest or other came to ask me to turn it down. All my favourite singers were girls. I was living a life of indolent voluptuousness interspersed with necessary drudgery. Like Emma Bovary, I was waiting for something to happen.

———

I returned Becky Sharp's books on time, and hoped to run into her at the library again, but of course I didn't.

Then one day I took Hetty for a walk to the local library where they were having a sale, and I went on a book spending-spree, and all I spent was two dollars … for ten books! And they were all in fairly good condition – not great, but the words were all there, and besides, I love old books.

My favourite was *The Bay of Noon*, by Shirley Hazzard, and I read it that very night. It was a wonderful watery book, full of dappled light. It was a paperback thirty years old, the pages brown and dry and drifting away from the spine like autumn leaves from a tree. It felt weightless when I held it in the palm of one hand. It was a mere scrap of a book, like a fruit peel, or a small bird, softly breathing. But through that novel I knew what it was like to live in an apartment on the Bay of Naples after World War II, to have a friend who was a sophisticated older woman, and to become involved with a man who was my friend's lover. And to see it, as the narrator did, all with the benefit of hindsight, sadly, nostalgically, because it was all in the past. I wondered if there would ever be for me a time like that, when I could look back on my life with acceptance and wisdom.

There was one part in particular I liked, on page 91, and I marked it for future reference. When Jenny, the narrator, goes to Gianni's flat, she says:

> *I don't think I ever saw all the rooms in Gianni's flat. When I said this to him he answered, 'In Italy one should try to have some rooms one doesn't have to enter. Like undeveloped aspects of one's personality.'*

Some nights, unable to sleep, I wandered barefoot through Samarkand's shadowy rooms. It was a house where the inside and the outside blended seamlessly, where rooms led onto broad verandahs and Nature was so close that the place seemed barely civilised. Mango leaves encroached through the windows, and bats squabbled in the branches outside. I would come across a green tree frog making its way across the bare wooden floor in search of cockroaches, or a mouse scuttling through a doorway, or a surprised-looking guest coming back late at night to encounter me, looking, I am quite sure, like the madwoman in the attic.

I felt that Samarkand must have captured something of every person who had ever been there – a molecule of breath, an atom of sloughed skin, an eyelash that had drifted into a seam in the upholstery, the echo of a voice, the insubstantial shimmer of a dream. I think that was what I was looking for, all the secret and unknowable things.

I imagined a hidden room that smelt faintly of oriental lilies, with faded rose wallpaper, a Persian carpet and an aspidistra that remained mysteriously watered. Because houses are like people, they have areas that remain mysterious, and that might never be known, no matter how you search.

––––––

At the end of that winter it rained, softly at first and then with a roar, driving fiercely onto the verandahs and pounding the house. Loose roofing iron clapped a rhythm to the deluge.

I love rain. You might have said that I was in my element. Hetty tugged at my breast, and it was sweetly satisfying, the way she stripped the milk from me. It was at that time, too, that my belly felt the pull of the moon and I menstruated for the first time since she was born. All of the liquid within or without me was in flux. One afternoon I went onto the verandah and saw that the river had broken its banks. Logs and debris rushed past on the brown water. Soon Samarkand would again be surrounded by floodwater. The old house yearned for it, I could tell, as if to be beset by flood was its natural condition.

Lil stood on the verandah watching. 'We'll be swept away!' she predicted, her eyes bright. The old drama queen! I knew that in the entire history of the place, floodwater had never come into the house.

But two of our guests decided to go to an evacuation centre that had been set up. The other two elected to stay. They were an Indian man named Dev and a woman called Pagan, who told us she was a Poet. She was pale and thin and freckled, with skimpy red hair, and I wished she was not quite so vapid-looking; she would give poets a bad name. Dev had flashing dark eyes and giggled a lot, and the two were almost each other's opposite in colouring and demeanour. They'd apparently not previously met, but I saw them later in the living-room together sipping tea. Pagan was reading his palm. There had developed a feeling of camaraderie brought on by the impending flood. The place felt like a houseboat.

———

Then we became more than a houseboat. We were an Ark!

First a dog arrived, just as the water started lapping at the bottom steps. She was a young border collie, thin and wet and shivering. I towelled most of the water from her fur, and as we had no dog food, I gave her some bread and butter and the bone from the previous night's leg of lamb, which she carried with her wherever she went.

Then, when water entirely surrounded the house, we acquired a small, dun-coloured domestic duck, who paddled up when the water reached its highest point, just below the level of the bottom floor. She came on board with a great flapping of wings and shaking of tail feathers, and then stood looking out at the flood as if she couldn't believe it (imagine a duck horror-stricken by the sight of water!).

It was strange and wonderful to be in a house that was lapped at by water and shut off from the rest of the world. Hetty sat on the bed listening to it with a look of awe and amazement on her face. And she was right to be awed – we were being visited by an act of the gods (which ones? I imagined the Greek ones – gods plural – gods multifarious and melodramatic).

The little border collie crept in (with her bone) through the open French doors of my room. She crouched at the entrance, and when I smiled at her she crept closer, and huddled on the floor near the bed.

I wondered who she was, and if anyone owned her.

I decided, in the meantime, to call her Tess.

We had two nights of being water-bound.

We don't usually serve any meal other than breakfast to our guests, but in the circumstances we could hardly starve them. And Dev turned out to be an inspired and enthusiastic cook. He took over the kitchen, and was wonderfully inventive with the various ingredients we had in store. Dev was short for a long polysyllabic name he refused to divulge on the grounds that we would never be able to pronounce it; his ethnicity may have been the reason he came up with delicious curried pasta dishes (we had no rice).

Cooking seemed an alien occupation to Pagan. She arrived in the kitchen to read out the collection of haiku about the flood she'd spent all day scribbling in her room, but Dev halted her after the first couple by holding up an imperious hand in the *Stop!* position.

'Pagan, dear,' he said. 'Could you possibly de-seed this cucumber for me? Never mind – I'll show you how. And in *this* bowl I want you to whisk up this apricot yoghurt – I'm afraid that's the only yoghurt we seem to have – and then over *here* there is a little pan for toasting coconut ...'

I left them to it. Lil's friends kept ringing to see if she was all right, so she was seldom off the phone. The rest of the time she stood on the verandah wrapped in her big brown cardigan, smoking and drinking cup after cup of tea.

The sun came out and the rain stopped, but the river didn't recede. A boat came to check on us and asked if we needed anything, or whether any of us wanted to leave. Lil told them that we were staying put, and asked for a cask of red wine. I asked for some food for Tess, and after a while they came back with several cans of Pal and bread and milk (but no wine). With her tummy full of food, Tess was very happy. She set herself up next to my bed and thumped her tail and smiled whenever I looked at her.

The duck was also quite content and stayed most of the time on the verandah with Lil, looking out at the flood. She ventured inside once to see what the rest of the house was like, leaving a trail of sloppy droppings, and hissed at me when I tried to shoo her out. I fed her on rolled oats and pearl barley and lettuce leaves.

Kate rang – she'd seen pictures of Lismore in the newspaper, with houses standing like islands in brown rushing water. She wanted to *be* here, and take part in the excitement of it all.

From the verandah, all you could see was muddy, swiftly flowing water and trees bowing under the weight of it. Logs and rubbish shot past. Lone belly boards surfed the rapids. A gutted refrigerator sailed majestically downriver on its back. A dead cow drifted by. Magpies sat in the tallest trees and looked down on it all, silent for once.

There's a smell that a flood gets, of earth and rotting vegetation, spicy and sweet and rotten at the same time, like an exotic soup. Afterwards, everywhere stinks of it, and there's a layer of silt over everything. You still find evidence of it months later – dried encrustations of mud on leaves or grass, and debris caught on fences and high in the branches of trees.

CHAPTER SIX

THE DUCK SET sail one morning. The water level had dropped, and she hopped carefully down to one of the lower steps, shook her tail, leaned forward to take a sip and paddled away. Later, when the water fell still further, Tess ran down and inspected the muddy, grassy area in front of the house. I half expected that, like the duck, she would keep going, but after sniffing around for a while she ran back up the steps and laid her nose in my hand.

The sun was out, and everything shone, even the receding brown water. Dev came out onto the verandah dressed only in jeans, towelling dry his long, black hair. He stood surveying the scene; with his smooth, brown chest he looked like a proud god. When Pagan arrived moments later, her face still bleary from sleep, he flashed a smile at her and said boldly, 'Would you like to go out and take a look around?'

She went inside to get dressed, and came back looking perkier than I'd ever seen her. I noticed then the beauty in her face. Going down the muddy steps she slipped, but Dev caught her arm, and they both giggled. When they reached the ground, they turned to wave cheerily to me. They sloshed away through the mud together.

There's always a feeling of celebration after a flood. People slide down muddy streets smiling at strangers when once they wouldn't have even nodded to them. Dev and Pagan came back with excited stories – of cars stalled in the water, and soggy carpets and appliances piled up in the streets, and people pushing mud from their houses with brooms. They'd seen a trailer full of caged chooks someone had rescued; one of them had laid an egg as they watched. Dev held out his hand and opened it like a magician – he'd taken it! (More smiles and giggles from the pair of them.)

That night they went out to get a meal at a pub. They invited me, but I could see they didn't really need company. I watched a little wistfully as they went off down the street again, their arms around each other.

Lil went out as well, borne away by a posse of friends who called for her in an ancient pumpkin-coloured Mercedes. So Hetty and Tess and I were left alone at Samarkand. It was so quiet I could hear the click of Tess's claws as she followed me about the house.

I wandered around from room to room, not able to settle to anything. I picked at leftovers from the fridge, and made some mashed vegetables for Hetty, which she hated. Hetty had always liked real food, not mushy stuff for babies. She loved nothing more than gnawing on a piece of steak, and even though she had very few teeth at that stage, she gnawed with her bare gums.

There was no meat, so I placated her with a jar of baby custard and stewed apples, which we shared. Afterwards, I went to my room (Tess following with her bone) and flipped through books, reading the choicest parts from the ones I loved best. In between, I built towers of blocks for Hetty so she could knock them down.

And finally, desperate to occupy myself, I put on some music and danced.

I'm not a dancer. I'm self-conscious and awkward and I know I look ridiculous. But sometimes that is what you must do with music, or it seems pointless. It's like seeing a shooting star and not gazing in wonder, or having a baby and not kissing it at every opportunity. Not moving to certain kinds of music is a crime against life.

So I danced, and Tess sat and watched me in a faintly embarrassed way (dogs are so conventional!). I picked up Hetty and whirled about with her in my arms for a bit. I danced for so long that I became breathless. Eventually, I became convinced that my dancing was graceful and wonderful and inspired. I ended up believing that I *could* dance.

I noticed that Tess was whining and shifting about, disturbed by something out on the verandah. The French doors were open, and I stopped dancing to see what she was looking at. In the puddle of light from my room, I saw someone standing outside in the dark looking in at me.

It was a woman in a long skirt made of creased grey silk, and a knobbly jacket. She was my height and build, with dark, crinkled hair worn loose to her waist. I feel sure I wore the same look of curiosity that she did, a kind of delighted recognition, because it was like looking into a dark mirror and seeing myself reflected.

———

The woman spoke first.

'Hello,' she said, and her voice had an edge of amusement to it. 'I'm sorry to disturb you, but I'm looking for a room. Is the manager in?'

I told her that I could help her, and she followed me downstairs. 'How many nights would you like?'

'Just one, for now.'

I selected a key and showed her to a room – one of the nicest, as it happened – that Lil had done up with freshly painted green walls and an old carpet of dusky faded red on the polished boards.

'It's perfect,' she said.

When I went to the window and pushed it up, cold night air came in, and with it the stink of the flood. She went to the window and leaned out. 'I love the night,' she said with a sigh. 'Don't you?'

I didn't reply, going out to the hall for the guest book to take down her particulars. She followed me, and collected an overnight bag she'd left at the entrance.

Her name was Maggie Tulliver, she said, smiling with what looked like practised charm.

'And do you have an address? Or phone number?' I asked, without much hope, as many of our guests don't. We attract a lot of nomads.

'None at the moment. I'm in transit. But I've been staying with people in Brisbane – I can give you their details.'

I took them down. I had Hetty on my hip, and while I wrote I noticed the woman frankly inspecting me. When I'd finished the paperwork she took herself and her bag off to her room.

I sat at the kitchen table with my chin propped on my fist, while Hetty crawled around on the floor. Tess sat at my feet with an awful, devoted, long-suffering look on her face that was already beginning to get on my nerves.

Maggie Tulliver had disconcerted me. I thought of the first impression I'd had of her. It was almost like looking at my double. We were both curvaceous women with long dark curly hair. But in the light, and on closer inspection, she wasn't so much like me. She was a good twenty years older, for a start. There were already strands of white in her dark hair.

I looked up when she came to the door in search of the bathroom; I'd forgotten to show her where it was.

'What's your baby's name?' she asked.

'Hetty,' I said cautiously, not wanting to give away too much about myself. I hate the way that living in a guesthouse can rob you of your privacy.

But something in me must have wanted to please her, and I offered her my own name soon afterwards without her even needing to ask. We were in the lounge at the time, and she had her head down inspecting the bookshelves for something to read. Coming up with a copy of *On the Road*, she threw back her head, tossing the hair away from her face in a gesture I knew well in myself. 'Sophie,' she repeated with satisfaction, as though I'd given her a gift.

She took herself to her room, and I didn't see her for the rest of the night. But very late, when I was almost asleep, I thought I heard someone singing. Getting up and going onto the verandah, I stood and listened. I remember shivering in the cold, but I couldn't go back inside, and stood watching the mist drift up from the river as the singing continued. The voice was beautiful, and arresting, but I remember most of all thinking how *confident* it seemed – to sing like that late at night, in a place where you were, after all, only a guest.

She was there at breakfast, but when I served her we didn't speak, except for her to say, 'Thank you.'

'Someone checked in last night,' I told Lil, as I took in her tray and whipped the curtains open.

'Oh, love, the light! The light!'

I pulled them closed again.

44

'I know. She was still up when I came in,' said Lil. 'She's coming back in a few weeks – booked in for long-term stay.'

When I went out, Maggie Tulliver was standing in the hallway looking at the ads for taxis and takeaway food on the noticeboard above the phone table. 'Oh!' she said, reaching up and taking down the strip of photos that Kate had taken in the booth. 'What a pretty girl.' She looked at me. 'Is this your sister? She looks so much like you. But everyone must tell you that.'

I took the photos from her. 'Actually, they don't,' I said, pinning them back on the board. She was correct about us looking alike. Only you had to know both of us well to see it.

She left while I was taking a shower. When I went to clean her room I found the house copy of *On the Road* on the bedside table. She had pulled out one of the long, white hairs from her head and used it to mark her place.

CHAPTER SEVEN

WITH MY LIFE at university tantalisingly close, I got into an irritable state of hating the whole world. In that mood, I took Hetty and Tess for a walk downtown, and we must have been a miserable sight. Hetty grizzled and gnawed at one hand, dribbling a trail of spit down her front. Tess trotted behind, tail down, at the end of a filthy bit of rope I was using as a lead.

I tramped along the street, preoccupied with my foul mood. As I passed the café where I used to work before Hetty was born, someone ran up behind me and touched me on the elbow.

'Sophie.'

And there was Becky Sharp, her little lobeless ears miraculously unchanged. In slim black slacks and white shirt, with a blue beret on her head. She slid her hands casually into her pockets.

I said her name aloud, hesitantly, as though I'd almost forgotten she existed, though in truth I think I'd called her to mind almost every day. She gestured towards the outdoor tables. 'Hey! Come and sit a while – do you have time?'

She was with a boy she introduced simply as Lawson, and whether that was his first or last name I couldn't tell. He was very tall, and dressed in a thick grey army coat. When he stood up to shake my hand he towered over me. Becky Sharp left us alone while she darted inside to order me a coffee, and he and I sat there silently, neither of us knowing quite what to say, though really I can only speak for myself. Perhaps he didn't want to talk.

But I liked him. He had the face of an ugly, faithful hound, with sincere eyes that turned down at the outer corners, and an immensely long nose that dominated a long face. Tess perked up at the sight of him; he smoothed back her ears firmly in a way she didn't mind at all, and when I let go of her rope she went to sit with her head in his lap.

Becky Sharp returned, and Lawson said he had to be going. He shook my hand again, patted Tess one last time, and departed. I had to call Tess back, as she had started to follow him, trailing her dirty rope over the footpath.

Becky Sharp and I looked at each other. It was difficult to know what to say to her, as I didn't want to say anything ordinary. She looked so extraordinary sitting there in the thin afternoon sunlight, her lovely pink mouth pursed in thought.

In the end, I said something absolutely commonplace:

'I took the books back.'

'I know.'

Taking a deep breath (I was so happy to see her I had forgotten to breathe), I added, 'I'm starting at uni after the break.'

'I'll probably see you about the place, then.'

I looked down into my coffee and took a sip.

Then, 'Have you ever cooked with Parisian essence?' I asked her. Only the Goddess, in all her wisdom, would know why I said something as pointless as that. I had noticed it the night before in our cupboard, and Lil had told me that its function was simply to make food brown.

'Um ... no,' she said. 'What exactly is it?'

I started to prattle. I do that when I don't know what to say and I want people to like me.

'It's just kind of brown. That's what it is. Brown stuff, to make food brown. It sounds exotic though, doesn't it? Essence of Paris. Who *wouldn't* want it in their food?'

Becky Sharp pushed her empty cup away to make room for an elbow, which she placed on the table, resting her chin in her hand. Her hair, which I think I said before was black, wasn't entirely black at all. Like my sister Kate's, it had green strands in it, and red.

'And some food really needs to be brown, doesn't it?' she said, with a smile. 'I'll look out for this Parisian essence.'

Hetty, still strapped into her pram, was starting to fuss. I picked her up and opened the buttons on my dress to feed her. Becky Sharp watched, frankly and openly, but it didn't worry me. What I hate is when people look at anything else *but* my breast.

She got up and went into the café and came back with blueberry muffins, which we ate silently while Hetty fed. It was nice not having to talk, and I felt most comfortable with Becky. She seemed to understand without being told how much I loved and needed food.

She took Hetty while I went off to the loo, and dandled her on her knee. When I came back she indicated that she was happy to keep her. And I can't remember what else we said to each other. I think we just sat there for a long while, looking at each other and smiling.

Eventually I said I had to go. And I got up and went, collecting up my baby and my dog, adjusting the pram, feeling slightly self-conscious at my disreputable-looking entourage.

I went home the long way, walking over the three bridges that cross Lismore's rivers (for Lismore is a place built on multiple converging rivers – no wonder it's such a place for floods). I thought about Becky Sharp almost all the way. Picking a flower that leaned out over a front fence (what was it? – let's say it was a gladiolus) I carried it as far as the bridge near the Winsome Hotel, where I leaned over and threw it into the river. I'm in the habit of throwing things into the river; it seems to me a gesture both practical and symbolic. A river brings, and it also takes away.

———

I know that at some stage I should give an account of myself: how I, an apparently not-too-badly educated girl, not too stupid (perhaps not too clever either), came to be blessed, as I see it, by a child at the age of twenty-one.

I remember this:

It was the middle of a morning in hot December; shafts of light shot from the surface of the river. Amazing to think that something as miraculous as Hetty could have her beginning with Marcus hugging a tree and exclaiming how good it felt.

I found my own tree to hug, and Marcus came over and embraced me against the slender, half-grown gum. Things went on from there. Slipping my knickers from underneath my skirt, I took Marcus by the shoulders and moved him so that I was on the outside and he was the one pressed up against the tree. We were hidden down near the riverbank, among weeds and tall flowering grasses. My knickers (red silky ones, my favourites) were scrunched up in one fist.

There was a woman picnicking with her two children over in the park, and I kept my eye on her at first to make sure she hadn't seen us, and then I got lost in the moment. Sex is essentially ridiculous when you think about it, but while you're actually doing it, it's not ridiculous at all, but lovely and essential. The thing I like is the way you reach a point where nothing else matters. There is that moment when time is suspended. Everything stops, and falls away.

We looked into each other's eyes the whole time. That was one thing I loved about Marcus, that he always kept his eyes open. Afterwards, I saw the woman in the park ushering her children away with an angry backwards glance. I also noticed with surprise that my knickers were still balled up into my fist.

And then I had to hurry to get to work on time, a wad of tissues stuck into my pants to collect the drips. I waited on tables all afternoon in a dreamy haze. I kept thinking of the Judith Wright poem, 'Woman to Man'. *The third that lay in our embrace* is the line that ran through my head. But there had been four of *us*: me, Marcus, the gum tree and Hetty. Hetty was as yet only there in her potentiality, but that's the point of the poem, isn't it?

In an idle moment, standing next to the sink and scoffing a piece of brioche that I pulled apart with sticky fingers, I thought about those animated diagrams of conception, with sperm wriggling their way towards the ovum. I wasn't sure how long that swim took, but sperm were small, so it must take some little time at least. In my mind, the baby was already the imperious little madam that Hetty in fact became. My womb was waiting for her. And although I knew in reality that it must be quite small (it had to be; it fitted in there somewhere between my fanny and my waist), in my imagination I saw that part of me as a place as large and as infinite as an entire universe, with its own constellations and weather. It was dark there, and beautifully patterned with stars.

———

That night Marcus stayed with me in my red-room at Samarkand. And though I knew that he would be gone in a few days, I didn't care because I had him with me here, now. I couldn't stop looking at him and marvelling. It was as if *he* was my baby, he was so exquisite, so perfect, so astonishing. I had this idea that there was a type of love that you didn't want to miss out on in your life, and I knew it was that type of love I was experiencing now. It was absolute, abandoned, and beyond sense or logic.

Marcus slept, and still my eyeless labourer toiled through the night, striving herself into being. *Are we there yet?* I asked her silently.

Not yet, not yet.

It was then that I felt fully the strength of my baby's will.

Then, when I was almost dead with exhaustion (I didn't want to miss the actual moment of my baby's arrival so I kept myself awake) I heard a bat fly into the room. It was one of those tiny bats that frequented the house, and was no bigger than a tiny mouse.

The sound of its wings stopped, and I switched on the reading light at the same instant that it alighted on the shade that hung in the middle of the room. As I watched, the bat took off, out through the doors leading to the verandah. The moment between its alighting and swooping away again was a long, breathless pause. It was like the swinging arc made by a trapeze artist in a circus, the releasing and grasping, another moment when time stood still.

And I know that it was at that moment, that split second as the bat pushed away from the lightshade, that a single spermatozoon, the winner of the race, reached its destination and Hetty came into being.

———

I had met Marcus only three days before. He was just another customer in the café where I worked, and he started a conversation by asking me what I did.

'What do you mean, what do I do?'

'For a living.'

'I work here.'

'No – I mean really…'

'I work here. Do you want pepper with that?' I brandished a tall grinder.

'You don't look like a waitress – you must do something else as well.' He was flirting with me, and I was pretending indifference.

'Really? What do I look like?'

'I dunno… an actress?'

It was at that moment I should have hit him with a line from Shakespeare or Edward Albee (or better still, the pepper grinder), but I never had the knack of saying something witty at the right time; it only ever came to me afterwards. I found myself agreeing to come to the pub that night where he had a gig. He said his name was Marcus Innocenti (*Sure*, I thought), and his band was called The Innocents.

I'd forgotten how viscerally live rock music hits you. How *loud* it is. The way the sheer volume of it pounds into your chest, taking you by force, storming right in and using your body as a sounding board.

I loved it; I could have sat there all night. I watched Marcus Innocenti and felt, rather than heard, the music that he made. I conceded that perhaps 'Innocenti' might be his real name after all because he *looked* Italian. That face, that nose, that dark hair, and the glance he shot me between songs that almost killed me. He looked anything but innocent, and that was the kind of boy I liked.

I hadn't dressed up, and still wore the outfit I'd worn at work, an old cotton dress and down-at-heel flats, ugly shoes that I hated; I called them my *licorice shoes* because of their unappetising dull black surface. Looking up from my horrible shoes, I made the fatal mistake of comparing myself with a slim, blonde girl in jeans and a skimpy top who seemed somehow connected with the band. She sipped at her beer with such a healthy unawareness of anyone else that I became painfully conscious that I can seldom lose myself like that in a crowd.

The music stopped and I got up and moved for the exit. I heard a voice say, over the microphone, 'I think we'll take a break,' and before I got to the door, Marcus Innocenti caught me up. And he looked at me with such an entreating expression that I couldn't help but go back with him. He led me to a seat in a corner and fetched us some drinks. As we sipped beer together I saw various girls I'd been at school with toss their hair and throw me hincty glances.

After the gig there was absolutely nowhere in Lismore for us to go, so we walked the darkened streets. It was early December, and some houses had Christmas lights out already. What did we talk about? I can't remember, and besides, who needed to talk? If I wanted conversation I'd read Leo Tolstoy. It was enough simply to be walking beside Marcus Innocenti, aware of every cell in his body.

We ended up at his motel. I hadn't been in many motel rooms in my life, and this one struck me as very depressing, with ugly furniture and expanses of brown curtain and carpet and bedspread. So far we hadn't touched each other, not on the walk, and not now. I sat on the end of the bed and drank a can of Passiona from the mini-bar. Marcus Innocenti made himself a cup of green tea. He sat beside me on the bed to drink it. I kicked off my shoes, and they lay there on the brown carpet looking very lost and ugly and alone.

He said, 'Tell me the story of your life.'

No one had ever said this to me before. It would never have crossed the minds of the boys I'd been with up till now.

Tell me the story of your life.

I looked at him, and it seemed as though he meant it. He smiled.

Marcus Innocenti wasn't your brooding, moody type. He was no Edward Rochester or Mr Darcy, and thank goodness for that. He smiled and laughed a lot, even though I couldn't remember afterwards exactly what he'd smiled and laughed about.

I took him at his word. I told him the story of my life. I told him everything, things I'd never told another soul. It took all night. It took till the dawn, lying all that time next to him on the bed, still not touching. When I'd finished he took my face between his hands and said, 'Do you know what? You're the funniest girl I've ever met in my life.'

We undressed each other and Marcus Innocenti examined every inch of my body. Under his scrutiny there wasn't one part of myself that I felt the need to cover up or feel ashamed of. He said, pinching the flesh tenderly between his fingers, 'You've got a fat back,' and it didn't seem that he was criticising, merely observing. He found the scar on my knee from when I'd fallen from a swing when I was four, and chided me gently for not telling him the *entire* story of my life after all.

Back in the days when I used to meet up with boys on the riverbank, after sex I always ended up reaching into my bag for my copy of *Anna Karenina*. I used to carry it with me to help me deal with boring moments in my life.

With Marcus Innocenti, the thought of *Anna Karenina* didn't even enter my mind.

CHAPTER EIGHT

THE DAY AFTER Hetty was conceived, Marcus and I found a set of old inks in an op shop. They were in small squat bottles, and were coloured crimson, vermilion, aquamarine, Prussian blue, chrome yellow, and dark, evil black.

The reds were as transparent as blood – all the colours but the black were transparent; we speculated that the other colours might have been from differently blooded people. We sat in my room and drew on large sheets of paper (all abstract stuff, just lines and squiggles, trying out the colours and dropping the ink from the stoppers, smearing them across the paper). And he told me about his family. His mother worked in a bank and his father sold appliances in a store. They lived in a squat brick house somewhere in Sydney's west and he had a little sister who played hockey and roller-skated. It all seemed so exotic – I longed to live his life, to go home to a mass-produced modern kitchen, up a path surrounded by unevenly mown lawn, to a family watching television and eating food they'd warmed in a microwave. There were people like that in Lismore, but their lives were unknown to me.

The name Innocenti was real, he said, only the Italian heritage was so long ago that no one remembered a thing about it. It had all been lost. He lived in the garage out the back of his parents' house, worked odd jobs when he wasn't doing gigs. They despaired of him, and I felt sad for him when he told me that, because I'd been allowed to glimpse an aspect of his life that wasn't all hope and glory and dazzling, beautiful noise.

That morning, drawing with the old inks, the late morning sunlight slanting through the doors, I thought that perhaps I had imagined I was now pregnant. The baby seemed a figment of my fevered imagination (and I was fevered – I was so filled with love for Marcus Innocenti that I was constantly giddy, and I hadn't slept properly for several nights in a row).

Marcus told me that he'd thought I must have invented the colourful past I'd related to him on that first night, but now, having seen Samarkand, he conceded that I might have been telling the truth. I smiled, and put three vermilion dots next to a Prussian blue square.

'Why paint your room *red*?' he asked, gesturing at the bright walls.

I shrugged. 'Why not?' I could only tell him so much about myself, after all. How could I tell him that the colour red represented my mother to me, and living in a red-room was a way of keeping her always with me when at that time I hadn't even reasoned that out for myself?

When we'd done enough fooling about with the inks, we lay next to each other on my bed and fooled around with each other. We compared the colour of our skins. The inside of my arm was the colour of a gardenia, he decided. I said his was polished wood. Both of us had hair of similar length, which made it easy to lay a hank of one across another. Though both were black, his hair was glossier than mine. And mine smelt filthy, he told me tenderly. It smelt of me, of my skin and sweat, as if I never used shampoo (and I didn't).

After Kate came in to offer to make us some lunch (but really to get a good look at Marcus) and I'd sent her away with an order for cheese on toast, Marcus said, teasingly, 'Do you *really* remember the day your sister was conceived? And your own birth?'

I nodded. 'I remember my own conception too,' I boasted.

He grinned and pinned me down, kissing me so hard that I could taste blood from where his teeth (they were very sharp) grazed the inside of my mouth.

———

He was so beautiful. That was the thing about him, his sheer beauty. And it would be a shame not to love beauty like that. People say that beauty isn't a virtue, but it is. What was it Oscar Wilde said? That only shallow people don't judge by appearances.

He wore make-up when he performed so that the bright lights didn't wash out the colour in his face, and wore it in the daytime as well (he was very tardy about taking it off at night, so that in my impatience to get at him, I copped toxic mouthfuls of lipstick and eyeshadow). Once, a waitress in a café paused in the middle of setting down our order to gushingly tell him he had beautiful eyes, and he responded with such innocent pleasure that I couldn't help but love him for it. His was such a simple soul: he loved praise and admiration, and was so charming that to be smiled upon by him was like a blessing. Knowing what I did about his family, I could see that he had constructed a persona for himself from nothing but his astonishing beauty and naturally generous impulses. We had that in common: both of us, in our different ways, had invented ourselves from the best part of our natures. And knowing that, how could I not feel optimistic about our child?

We talked and talked, and thought in euphoria that we had *everything* in common. (Now, in retrospect, I see we had very little in common, but when you're in that state of being miraculously in love any small similarity seems pre-ordained and stupendously significant. 'Really?' you say. 'You like that too? That's amazing. So do I!' and 'You too? *I* feel that way!' All your conversations go like that.)

I knew that he would soon be gone, and I wanted to remember him. Perhaps Hetty was a way of memorising him. But when I look at her now, I can see that she is her own self, that despite my efforts, Marcus Innocenti has eluded me.

I wanted to capture a part of him, and I know that was wrong of me. I didn't ask him if he wanted to father a baby.

But then, if he didn't, he should have taken more precautions.

———

I had always wanted Hetty. There was never one moment when I wished her away.

And I didn't want Marcus to go. In the week we'd been together, even though I knew he would soon be moving on, I hadn't really believed it. I hadn't wanted to think about it.

But in the end, he was gone suddenly.

They left before dawn, him and the rest of the band. If I haven't described the other band members, it's because they're not important in the story of Marcus and me. But on the last morning, there they were in the car park at the motel, loading stuff into the van: the hairy rhythm guitarist, the chunky bass player, the nondescript drummer and the blonde girl I'd noticed the first night, who seemed to be some kind of manager. I saw then that they were realer to him than I was, and their lives were more connected.

When they were packed, Marcus hugged me tightly, told

me it had been fun, and got into the van. They roared away. He hadn't offered to keep in touch, or asked for an address and phone number (but he knew where I lived, didn't he? I clung to that thought for a long time).

His leaving had been so lacking in ceremony that I felt a creeping sense of humiliation. It was only just dawn, and there I was standing in a motel car park in a summer dress and my broken-down old licorice shoes. I felt exposed and alone. It wasn't cold, but I needed a coat to snuggle into. I wanted some kind of shell or carapace to armour myself with.

But I had only my mind, which has always been my saviour and great protector, and conjures up reserves of steely determination on most of the occasions that I need it.

The sun came up. I walked through the deserted streets in a light that showed nothing, including myself, to advantage. Everything was unutterably dreary, every crack and blemish in the world exposed. Instead of going straight home to Samarkand, I walked out onto the bridge at the end of the street (which later became *our* bridge, mine and Hetty's, on our regular morning walks). I removed the horrid licorice shoes that I'd worn the night I met Marcus and tossed them down into the water. I heard them fall in. Plop. Plop.

Then I walked home barefoot.

CHAPTER NINE

WHEN I WAS pregnant with Hetty, I never thought beyond that time. I didn't imagine that I would have another life afterwards that would mean sometimes leaving her behind.

'Live your life,' Lil had always urged us. So on the first day of university, I slung two bags over my shoulder (one each for Hetty and me), hefted her onto my hip, and went to go out the door. But beset by sudden fear and indecision, I turned back to Lil, who'd been standing there seeing us off.

Her face stoic, she reached out and plucked a piece of fluff from my cardigan (a symbolic gesture if ever there was one, as there were many bits of fluff and stray hairs forever about my person), and spat on the corner of a handkerchief to wipe a smear of Vegemite from Hetty's cheek.

You'll do.

This time she didn't need to say the words aloud. It was what she'd always told us as she prepared Kate and me for each small step out into the world. '*You'll do.*' And we had always believed that we would.

———

As I'd feared, when I left Hetty at the university childcare centre she howled, with great roars of rage and sorrow. She was in the arms of a carer named Jill, tossing herself about like a ship in a storm. I hesitated, tugged back by guilt and pity. 'Just go,' said Jill. 'She'll be fine. You'd be amazed how quickly she'll get used to it. These tears will be gone in a few minutes.'

I made my way across the campus, blocking out the memory of her screams by thinking of Kate at Sydney University. She had described ancient weathered sandstone, dim old corridors and azalea-filled courtyards. I thought how that would suit me far more than all this brick and concrete, linked by expanses of lawn with gum trees full of screeching parrots.

I was anxious about becoming a student again. Since leaving school, the only new thing I'd learnt had been how to write shorthand. I'd taught myself from an old textbook I'd found at Samarkand. I enjoyed the way shorthand was a kind of code, known only to the initiated. I felt I was part of a secret society, of sorts. Now, at least, it might come in handy for taking notes.

In the lecture theatre I took a seat close to the back; I'd been so anxious to be on time that I was early. As I watched the other students make their way in groups into the tiered theatre I realised that because it was mid-year most of them would already know each other.

People trickled in, and I noticed how informal everyone was, leaning across casually to cadge pens or paper from friends; *they* weren't looking at everyone, or wondering whether people were looking at them. (But of course, no one was observing me. I was invisible because I was of no interest to anyone; why should anyone bother to notice a new student, a part-timer at that?)

I opened my lecture pad, and with the flat of my hand caressed the beautiful blank page. So I used to smooth my workbooks at school when I was a child, writing with my face almost on the page, watching the words spool magically away from my pen.

The lecturer spoke of the revolution in thought that took place in the nineteenth century, and how that influenced the way we think today. She talked about Mary Wollstonecraft, and the rights of women, and the influence of that on the Brontë sisters and George Eliot. She asked us to consider how might Wollstonecraft's thinking have influenced *Jane Eyre*, and why *Pride and Prejudice* still had such a wide readership.

Looking back at my notes from that day, I find things like: *Marxist-Feminist analysis of the text!! What does this mean?*

The lecturer spoke of Freud, and the idea of the unconscious … the birth of modernist art … and the madwoman in the attic …

I took it all down, and afterwards went to the university library, and put in an application for a library card. Going up the stairs, I remembered the day Becky Sharp had scooped Hetty up into her arms and strolled away; the poetry of her stride. In truth, I longed to see her again, and hoped to run into her at any minute.

But I didn't. In the meantime, there was the luxury of being a legitimate library user. I drank in the peace, and looked through the shelves to see what I'd borrow when my card was processed. Then I sat in a carrel and read through the study guide.

I had no other lectures that day, and just before lunch I went to collect Hetty, who scowled at me the whole time I fed her. On the way home in the bus she fell asleep against my shoulder, and I had to wake her up again to put her into her pram.

The next day brought a letter from Kate. I had the day off, and though the weather was still wintry, I lay out on the verandah in the hammock to read it – such a lovely long letter, full of gossip and description.

Every day Kate fed the ducks on the lake next to the university; the park was either full of solitary people like herself, or couples kissing. *I have never been kissed!* she wrote. *Or not in that way.*

But she'd met a boy, Myles, in one of her English tutorials. She described him in detail (*very pretty, with a face like a lost angel* she wrote). And it seemed that this Myles *liked all the right writers*, Sylvia Plath, and Virginia Woolf, and Jack Kerouac. And he listened to Ella Fitzgerald and Bessie Smith, who were black women singers that Kate had never even heard of before, but he was going to invite her to his place to listen to them some time (O, Kate!).

If I hadn't lost that letter I could write it down word for word. I swung in the hammock as I read, holding the letter in one hand so it fluttered like a little flag in the breeze. And as I finished each page I dropped it carelessly onto the floor where Hetty seized it with squeals of delight, scrunching it up in her fists and sucking on it.

As I finished the last page (there was much, much more about this Myles, and about a job she'd just got cleaning in a motel), I dropped it onto the floor and lay back with my eyes closed, thinking about Kate. Hetty became intent on pressing one of the pages of the letter into my ear, and as I opened my eyes to fend her off I found myself face to face with Maggie Tulliver again.

―――――

'I seem always to catch you at an awkward moment,' she said. Her voice still had an edge of sly amusement to it that made me self-conscious, but at the same time I wanted to be in on the joke with her. I knew that after her one night at the time of the flood she was meant to be coming back again, so she must only have recently arrived.

Hetty dropped the piece of paper she'd been trying to cram into my ear and scooted away on her bottom. She went over to the barricade I'd put at the top of the stairs and pulled herself to her feet, gesturing towards the tops of the trees and the river as though to draw our attention to their magnificence. I thought that if she ever acquired the art of speech Hetty would make a grandiloquent orator. She had the knack of the grand, the amplified, the eloquent gesture.

'She needs to learn how to crawl,' said Maggie Tulliver, in a detached voice. 'That bottom-scooting's an easy way to get about, but it won't do her any good in the long run.'

'What do you mean?' I felt cautious and hostile. Was she telling me that Hetty was *lazy*?

'Crawling is critical to a baby's development. It wires the brain to cross-pattern.'

I must have still been looking deeply suspicious.

'It establishes a crossover flow of energy,' she explained. 'All sorts of movement, even walking, will be easier for her if she learns to crawl first.'

'She's worked out that way of getting about by herself,' I said sullenly. 'I know it looks sort of awkward and lopsided, but it seems to work for her.'

'For now. But she'll get on better later on if she crawls properly first. You can teach her by showing her, you know.'

And she got down on her hands and knees and started to crawl. Hetty looked at her with interest – she had a way of regarding everything new she encountered as something she might need to know.

'*You* show her,' Maggie Tulliver urged.

Feeling foolish, I got out of the hammock and into a crawling position. I called out, 'Hetty! Watch this.'

She sat holding onto her toes, smiling at me indulgently. I crawled up to her and lifted her into the correct position. She sat right back down onto her bottom.

'Try again.'

This time Hetty started imitating me. She crawled a few paces, arms and legs working in opposition.

'Good girl, Hetty!' I said. She sat up on her bottom again and grinned at me.

We spent ages crawling around with Hetty, and by the end she was starting to get the hang of it. She thought it was a marvellous game we were playing with her.

Lil came out to see what was going on. We explained to her and she said, 'Well I never. In my day, crawling was just crawling and babies seemed to manage all right.'

Maggie Tulliver and I looked at each other and smiled.

'Is that a letter from Kate?' said Lil, noticing the pages floating about on the floor. She picked them up and started to smooth them out, tutting about the dreadful state they were in. She went inside, taking the letter with her. 'Read away,' I said with a flourish, as she disappeared. Anything from Kate was Lil's as far as Lil was concerned.

Maggie Tulliver left then as well, and it was only after she'd gone I realised I hadn't known why she'd come up to the top floor in the first place, as it was our private part of the house.

———

I saw her again on Sunday night.

When I can't sleep, I go to a sitting place on a short, secluded flight of steps that runs from the bottom floor at the back of the house to the garden. I sit on a step near the ground, next to a patch of fragrant mint. If Hetty's asleep, I take her with me bundled up in a straw carry-basket, where she lies charmingly like baby Moses in the bulrushes.

That night there was a woman sitting in my exact spot; she turned around as I stood at the top of the stairs with the basket, hesitating. It was Maggie Tulliver. 'Have a seat,' she said carelessly, over her shoulder.

I made my way down the steps and sat, not beside her, but a couple of steps above, with Hetty's basket next to me.

Maggie Tulliver said, 'At times like this I miss smoking. Sitting still, looking at the dark, and doing nothing.' She reached down and picked a sprig of mint, pinching it between her fingers. 'I gave it up ages ago because of the singing. I'm in the music school up at the uni – doing voice.'

I said, 'I'm studying literature and writing. I'm only part-time at the moment, so I'm doing the literature first. "Introduction to written texts" it's called.'

Maggie Tulliver laughed. 'Don't you love the crazy subjects they teach?' she said, with more than a hint of mockery in her voice.

I hesitated. Actually, I thought it sounded an interesting subject, but I didn't feel up to defending it.

I usually try to keep myself apart from the guests, but the experience with Dev and Pagan (who had ended up leaving together) had made me think that perhaps I should try to be more open to the people who stayed with us. It might be interesting, and companionable.

'Would you like a cup of tea?' I asked.

'You offering to make it?'

I got to my feet. 'If you could just watch Hetty for me ...'

She threw the basket a glance that spoke of a high disregard for babies. Despite her knowing that thing about crawling, I got the feeling she didn't really like them.

That was disappointing, because I'd begun to have a curious feeling of intimacy with her. Perhaps it was simply the effect of the night, and our proximity to each other in the dark. She was so close I could smell her. Some women smell overwhelmingly of floral perfume, but Maggie Tulliver has a sour, almost citrus-like odour that intrigued me.

I brought back the tea and we sat there sipping it. Finally, Maggie Tulliver leaned over and tipped the last of hers into the mint, and it seemed to be a signal that she was leaving. Impulsively, I said, 'How about I cook you dinner some time?' (As I've said, we don't, as a rule, serve dinner to our guests.)

She said, 'That'd be nice.'

'How about tomorrow night?' I knew Lil planned to be out with friends, so we'd have the kitchen to ourselves.

'What time?'

'About seven?'

That night I took Hetty into bed with me. She had a cot, but I often slept with her beside me. I listened to her murmurs that were so like the words she couldn't yet say when she was awake. I wondered what colours her dreams contained, and whether she was remembering or imagining. I loved the solidity of her presence, and the intensity with which she slept. I loved it that when I woke in the morning she was often staring right into my face.

CHAPTER TEN

THE NEXT TIME I left Hetty at child care, I wondered where my normally sunny-natured child had gone. Surely the fairies must have been, and substituted a changeling with a foul temper in her place. I stood and watched helplessly as she went purple with fury, bubbles of spit and snot all over her face. Her screams rent the air so rudely that other mothers looked askance.

'Just go,' said Jill. 'She'll be fine.'

I went.

The lecture hall was a refuge. The murmur of voices, the soft carpets, the discreet lighting, the cushioned seats and the air of calm expectancy made me relax. Already, I belonged there a little more than I had the last time. I dropped a pen, and the person in the seat near me retrieved it. He noticed my page of shorthand scrawl. 'Nifty!' he said with a smile.

That day the lecture was on *Jane Eyre*.

I learned that one female critic at the time said that if she had been Jane Eyre she'd have *shot* Rochester because of his deceit (whereas *my* impulse would have been to run off and live in sin with him since he wasn't legally free to marry).

The lecturer spoke of the sadomasochistic forces at work in *Jane Eyre*, the cruelty Jane was subjected to, how she was like a caged bird. I took notes dutifully, as most students do. She suggested that her spirit was corrupted by the cruelty. *Abandonment, loss, defencelessness*, were the words I scrawled in shorthand on my pad in the interests of scholarship, as though these were mere words and had nothing to do with me.

She finished up with this quotation from the book, the part where Jane is locked in the fearsome red-room:

> *'Besides,' said Miss Abbot, 'God will punish her: He might strike her dead in the midst of her tantrums, and then where would she go? Come, Bessie, we will leave her: I wouldn't have her heart for anything. Say your prayers, Miss Eyre, when you are by yourself; for if you don't repent, something bad might be permitted to come down the chimney and fetch you away.'*

'I'll leave you with that,' said the lecturer, with a smile that came close to sadism. She closed her book.

Something came over me. I was a child again, and had been left alone in an empty flat, thinking I must have done something wrong to deserve it.

Getting to my feet, I pushed in front of people in my urgency to get away. I found myself crying (crying! I never cry!) as I raced down the paths through the university to the childcare centre. I thought only of Hetty, of how alone, how abandoned she must feel. Her screams had been heartfelt, and real.

When I reached the centre, Jill led me through to where Hetty was; her gestures cautioned me to observe quietly.

And there was my baby, sitting in the middle of a cluster of children. A little boy of about three was talking to her, and she was smiling at him and drooling, so clearly charmed by his conversation that she was lost in it. He leaned forward and gave her a hug; she squealed and grabbed him by the ears in her joy. She sat there in her old-fashioned white nightie with embroidered flowers round the neck, looking exquisitely happy.

I left without her even noticing I'd been there, and went to the library, where I sat and looked over my notes from the lecture: *abandonment, loss, defencelessness.*

―――――――

That was the night I'd offered to cook for Maggie Tulliver. I'm not a natural cook, unlike Kate, who can turn the compost heap in our laughingly named vegetable crisper into a feast.

But I was happy, frying onions and garlic, chopping vegetables and finding all kinds of interesting flavourings in the cupboards. The main course was a kind of vegetable stew, with tinned tomato soup to start (with a dollop of sour cream), and Kate's dessert specialty for afterwards. (For the record, it's a sheet of frozen puff pastry with the edges crimped up, with sliced raw apple, brown sugar and cinnamon piled on top, then baked to caramelised perfection. I've heard that some people like a few recipes in a novel, so be my guest. Cook away!)

I fed Hetty while I was cooking. She was tired after her day at child care, and afterwards I put her to bed in our room. Then I sat with Tess at my feet in the kitchen and waited for Maggie Tulliver.

And she never turned up! At the point where I knew she was never going to appear I reheated the soup, because despite my humiliated, stood-up feeling, I was very hungry. After I'd eaten, I went to my room and seethed. I imagined a Maggie Tulliver doll, which I could stick pins into. Then I told myself it didn't matter. What was one dinner, in a whole life of dinners? *One of these days you'll laugh about it.* Isn't that what people said? I didn't think I would, as there was nothing funny in the situation at all. One of these days, I would simply forget about it.

I heard Lil arrive back while I was trying to get to sleep. There was a great slamming of car doors and raucous laughter as her friends dropped her off. The conversations those old women had late at night after a few drinks would make a Russian sailor blush!

Much later, I heard footsteps that might have belonged to Maggie Tulliver. I thought it ridiculous that I should be nursing hurt pride over someone I barely knew. But there it was, sitting in my chest like a stone.

Chapter Eleven

At breakfast, Maggie Tulliver apologised casually for forgetting the dinner. She had clean forgotten, she said. I replied that it hardly mattered; that I myself had almost forgotten she was coming, but inside I still nursed my humiliation. I made a vow to have nothing to do with her in future.

It was a non-uni day, so I did housework and read my lecture notes. That is a sentence filled with dull despair, if ever there was one. By the afternoon, when I took Hetty and Tess out for a walk, I was filled with discontent with my life, which seemed flat and predictable. The weather had turned blustery and cold. Everything that day was grey. I had to get a few things from the supermarket, but first, in an attempt to cheer myself up, I called in at the city library and borrowed one of my favourite books from the stack.

The stack is one of those no-go areas of the library that the librarians disappear into and emerge with the item you requested. In the case of our city library, this is not because the books are special, but because they're so old and tattered that no one ever reads them. I suspect it's the last stage before they get chucked out.

The book I requested was *Oscar Wilde, Selected Works*, edited by a Richard Aldington in 1946. It was clear from his preface that Mr Aldington disapproved strongly of Oscar Wilde's personal life, and didn't even appear to like his writing very much. I was surprised that he even bothered to edit the book. But as it contained writing that I hadn't seen elsewhere, I was thankful that he had.

So by 1946, Oscar Wilde still hadn't been forgiven, though he'd died at the turn of the century. Through his drama, he exposed the hypocrisy of late Victorian life; at first people loved him for it, and then they turned on him. He was imprisoned for his homosexuality, made a scapegoat really, and prison destroyed him, it really did – his spirit and his health. And then when he was released he was so reviled and shunned that he exiled himself to Paris, where he died soon afterwards.

I wonder if he ever had an inkling that long after he was dead, there would always be people who embraced and loved him? Perhaps he did. 'If one tells the truth,' he said, 'one is sure, sooner or later, to be found out.'

———

Putting the book into my bag, I made my way to the supermarket. Despite getting my hands on a favourite book, I was in a particularly sour mood. After the gloom outside, the supermarket seemed supernaturally bright, a cacophony of clattering trolleys, muzak and voices. I emerged thinking that you would need to be a poet to find anything lovely about Lismore that day.

You find this ugly, I find it lovely – didn't Kenneth Slessor write that about William Street in Kings Cross? And William Carlos Williams wrote about white chickens and red wheelbarrows and rainwater; he wrote about broken green glass in the cindery earth behind hospitals.

Even William Carlos Williams would have been hard-pressed to find anything to write about in Lismore that day.

As I walked, I saw that the hill above the town was filled with really awful houses, and the Worker's Club, all brick, had not a window in it. Next to it was an enormous new motel painted a particularly ugly magenta. I passed depressed-looking people in trackpants and thin polar-fleece jackets, ugly businessmen in ugly suits, and every second person was talking into a mobile phone. With disgust I noted service stations, all concrete and garish signs, car yards, and a pitiable dead pigeon in the gutter.

And then we came to the filthy, weed-infested river, which I crossed on a bridge I don't often use. On the other side of the bridge was a roundabout with a fake windmill, and an old timber structure stuck in the middle of it. Here the houses were old (usually I like that) but their peeling paint that day was particularly depressing. Other old houses had been done up, but in such an ugly way that it was worse than neglect. The defunct railway line was surrounded by dry, weedy grasses. I saw galvanised-iron sheds with gravel surrounds, so stark that I wanted to fall weakly to my knees in despair. Then more car yards, dog shit in gutters; a man who was unravelling in every conceivable way rode a bicycle with a milk crate on the back, the pavements were cracked, and there were cars everywhere.

I hated all of it.

And then I came to the stone lions.

They were at the entrance to a small park next to the old railway station. The park had a couple of shade trees, some swings, and neatly mown grass. It was fenced with timber palings painted in heritage colours, cream and brown and dark green – all ugly colours, especially when put together like that.

The lions stood on either side of the gateway; and sat on all fours on top of small concrete plinths, in a classical lion pose.

They, too, were made of concrete, and had been painted cream once, but the colour had almost all worn away. They were such small lions, no bigger than a cocker spaniel, with nothing majestic about them. Their blunted muzzles were chipped and worn.

I sat down on the back of one of the lions and reached into my bag, retrieving the book I'd borrowed. I turned to my favourite bit, a letter that Oscar Wilde had written to his mother from Venice:

> *After dinner we went to the theatre and saw a good circus. Luckily a wonderful moon – we landed from our gondola coming from the theatre at the Lion of St Mark. The scene was so romantic that [? it] seemed to be an artistic scene from an opera. We sat on the base of the pillar – on one side was the Doge's Palace, on the other the King's Palace – behind us the campanile – the water steps crowded with black gondolas – and a great flood of light coming right up to us across the water – every moment a black silent gondola would glide across this great stream of light and be lost in the darkness.*

I closed the book, and sniffed with shameful self-pity. It all sounded so beautiful. And look at where *I* was! Lismore was not Venice, and it would never be.

The Lion of St Mark. The Doge's Palace. It sounded so grand.

But Oscar wasn't trying to make people feel envious. What surrounded him was wonderful, and he *saw* that it was.

And then it struck me why I loved Oscar Wilde so much. The fundamental spirit in his work is joy. I thought of his lovely plays, and the way they made me laugh. *'I like to keep a diary. It gives me something sensational to read on the train.'*

Something gave way inside me. I looked at Hetty. *She* didn't hate our surroundings; she liked going for walks, and was looking about with interest. Tess, too, seemed happy to be out and about. She sat wagging her tail at me.

I looked across at the battered little concrete lion, companion of the one I sat on, and felt huge affection for it. It wasn't the Lion of St Mark. But it was *our* lion. Across the road I could see a service station, a tattoo parlour, a butcher shop, a laundromat, and Dr Dirt of Dunoon (Dirt Bike Specialist).

I loved it all.

And at the edge of my vision, as if he'd been conjured by my love for the place where I lived, was Oscar. Very tall, in a long coat, he stood watching me.

With a camera?

———

Of course, it wasn't Oscar Wilde, it turned out to be the boy I'd met with Becky Sharp in the café that day. I stood up.

'What are you doing?' I called out indignantly, hands on my hips like a fishwife, and my voice as shrill.

The boy slung the camera over one shoulder and approached me.

'You're Sophie, aren't you?' he said, holding out his hand. 'I'm Lawson. We met the other day?'

'I remember,' I told him, whisking Hetty out of her pram. She'd started to grinch at the sound of my furious voice.

'Well?' I said. 'How about asking permission first? Or apologising for *taking* my photo without me knowing?'

'I'm sorry,' he said. 'If I ask permission first it loses its spontaneity. The photo is never as good. Look, come and sit down with me a while.'

I consented to go into the park with him, where we sat on a bench under a spreading tree.

'Actually, I do often feel guilty about taking pictures of people without asking. But I want them,' he said simply. It struck me that he was as callous as a child. He shrugged, as though it couldn't be helped. 'Sometimes the picture seems the most important thing.'

I didn't reply, but now I understand him perfectly; I feel the same way about writing.

Delving into my shopping bag, I took out a packet of shredded wheatmeal biscuits and gave us all one. Lawson looked at the biscuit I handed him as if it was a foreign object. Tess gulped hers down at once and sat looking at Lawson with an expression that managed to look both put-upon and melancholy.

His hands were huge and bony. He had a large frame, and was bony all over. The skin on his face had the texture of fine sandpaper, or of having been sprinkled lightly with salt. If I leaned over and licked it, that would be the taste of him.

Lawson broke his biscuit in two and gave one half to Tess, who lapped it into her mouth. After a moment, he fed her the other half.

'Can I look at them?' I nodded towards his camera. 'The pictures of me.'

'It's not digital,' he said, lifting up the large, old-fashioned camera for me to see. 'It's film. I'll let you know when I've printed them.'

We started walking. There was a row of shops, one with brightly coloured pennants streaming high up in the wind. Then came a row of old timber houses, built on stilts because of the floods. On the other side of the road, next to the railway line, were fig trees with bright green leaves in thick crowns, like a child's drawing of trees.

My day had changed completely. It glowed. Every house we passed looked as though exotic secret lives were being lived inside it. We came to the twin bridges, and we crossed the first one and arrived at the Winsome Hotel.

Lawson gestured down Bridge Street and said, 'I'm going to head down here.'

'I'll see you, then.' I prepared to cross the second, my usual bridge.

After only a few steps Lawson ran to catch me up. 'I forgot – we're having a party on the weekend.' He felt in his coat pockets and found a scrap of paper to scrawl on. I put it in my bag without glancing at it. 'It'd be nice to see you there.'

'I don't know whether I'll come. Not much of a party person.'

But he ignored that. 'Arrive late. We can never seem to get going early.'

He gave Tess a last pat, and she went as if to follow him; I had to tug hard on her rope to make her come with me.

CHAPTER TWELVE

ON THE DAY I attended my first tutorial, dropping Hetty off at child care was the easy part. She was insultingly ready for me to leave her, and looked with smug cheerfulness at all the children who greeted her warmly. She was one of the few really little ones there, and already the older children spoilt her.

In the classroom, we sat in a semi-circle facing the front, in two rows. I took a seat at the back. Outside, the hillside had been cut away, and the view was of a clay bank covered with weeds. It was such an unromantic university, all brick and concrete and square edges, with weeds and rainforest trees instead of ivy.

First of all, there was a certain amount of clarification regarding essay questions and so forth to be gone through. As part of the assessment, we had to construct and answer our own question, and one suggested in the study guide took my eye: *The possibility that writing can be female in style.*

Then the tutorial proper started. The tutor talked about what could not be spoken by women in nineteenth-century literature, and the way the text of *Jane Eyre* could be seen as a palimpsest (meaning something rubbed smooth, so that something may be written over the top). In a subversive way, it speaks what cannot be spoken.

'The female voice is duplicitous,' he said.

'Women never say what they mean,' quipped a male student, and everyone laughed.

I looked at the portrait of Charlotte Brontë on the cover of my book, so small and plain and poverty-stricken. I've heard she had bad teeth. She was proud and sharp-tongued; I don't think she was *nice*. I like that. She wanted so much, yet so little, really – love and sex and independence, things that many women today would think of as their right. But at least, through the power of her writing, she could allow the women in her books to get what *she* wanted. Though they got it only sometimes, and in roundabout ways. She must have been a realist, for all her gothic overtones.

It was a two-hour tutorial, and we had a break mid-way. As people got up to stretch their legs, I heard a girl say softly to her neighbour with awe, 'Imagine how many people have read this book. Millions ... '

Most people went out of the room; I stayed where I was, and struck up a conversation with a girl who'd also stayed behind. Her name was Phoebe. She was even older than me: twenty-eight, she said. She told me she'd been longing to come to university for years, and now that she had, it was everything she'd thought it would be.

She was one of those people who are pure pleasure to look at. She had black hair and red lipstick, and around her neck was a string of large red beads. I liked her friendliness, and her care for her appearance struck me as being extremely considerate. I myself have no thought for those who must view me. My hair is often a mess and I leave my clothes all over the floor of my room so they are perpetually crinkled and quite often not even very clean.

After the break, we divided up into groups, and our task was to look closely at certain parts of *Jane Eyre*. Phoebe and I were with two other girls, and were allotted the scene where Jane is locked in the red-room.

We looked at the symbolism in the description of the room: the bed 'stood out like a tabernacle in the centre'; it has curtains of red damask; so do the windows. The carpet is red, and the table covered with a crimson cloth. The room is chilled and silent, and seldom entered. Her uncle had died there. Everything in the description speaks of death and blood and anger.

Jane Eyre sees herself reflected in the mirror of a wardrobe; she looks to herself like a phantom. It is in the red-room that Jane fights an internal battle between the light that others cast her in and her sense of herself and feelings of injustice. Her brain is in tumult, and her heart in insurrection. *'I could not answer the ceaseless inward question – why I thus suffered; now, at the distance of – I will not say how many years – I see it clearly.'*

Afterwards, we reported on what we'd discussed. To my surprise, the boy who'd made the stupid quip about women never saying what they mean spoke with empathy. He said that the part about Jane being locked in the red-room was something that everyone could identify with.

'It's one of your greatest fears as a child. Being locked in a room … and in the dark.'

Tears sprang to my eyes. I wiped them away, hoping no one had seen. Then my breasts started to leak milk. I murmured my excuses and went out.

In the privacy of a toilet cubicle I allowed the liquid part of myself full rein. I wept and wept, not fully knowing why I was crying. I stuffed tissues into my bra to catch the milk, and then noticed that there was blood on my underpants. My body seemed intent on betraying me at exactly the time when I needed my intellect. I wondered how I could ever spend years at university if my first tutorial brought me to this.

I went out to the washroom and splashed water on my eyes. Phoebe came in as I was rubbing my face with a paper towel. 'Are you okay?' she asked.

'Yes,' I told her. 'I am now.' I glanced at myself in the mirror; I looked terrible. My eyes were red from crying, my face mottled, my hair a tangled mess. 'Is the tutorial over?' I asked, and she nodded.

She started to reapply her lipstick, looking into the mirror, but keeping an eye on me as well. 'Do you want to come for a coffee? That's if you don't have anything else on.'

'No, I'm through for the day. But I think I should get down to the childcare centre and feed my baby. I'm leaking.' I indicated the damp spots on the front of my dress.

'Oh!' she said. 'You have a baby. That must make it difficult sometimes.' She put away her lipstick. 'But we'll get together another time, yeah?' She smiled at me as I went out.

I sat in a quiet corner of the childcare centre and fed Hetty, thinking how easy it would be if I weren't a student.

I thought about the essay topic: *The possibility that writing can be female in style.*

If I were to attempt to answer that it would mean many hours of research, and more thinking than I'd been used to. I wondered if I was up to it. I contemplated an afternoon in the library taking notes, and was very tempted to pack Hetty up there and then and take her home. The thought brought a smile to my lips, and Hetty dropped my nipple and smiled back at me.

82

But two minutes later she was asleep at my breast. I considered my options. I thought of what our lives would be like if I *didn't* get a university degree. Things still weren't too bad while Hetty was a baby, but I depended on Lil to an alarming degree – she still provided a roof over our heads, for instance, and while we were at Samarkand we were never going to actually *starve*. But children cost, and I didn't want to support Hetty all her life on a waitress's wage, or worse, on the pension.

And very quietly, and with very little guilt, I carried the sleeping Hetty to the cot they'd allotted her, tucked her into it, and made my way back up the hill to the library.

CHAPTER THIRTEEN

ON THE NIGHT of Lawson's party I set out at about nine-thirty with Hetty asleep in the pram and Tess at my heels. I hadn't dressed up for a party; actually, I wasn't sure if I'd end up even going to it. I planned to wander in that direction and see what happened.

The path under the fig trees was secluded and hushed; as I came out from that friendly darkness and headed towards the town, the lit-up shopping streets with cruising cars seemed another country altogether. I crossed the bridge. Underneath the river gleamed blackly. As I passed the Winsome Hotel, talk and laughter shot out like bursts of gunfire.

Down the street from the pub were the occasional darkened old shops, with houses set between them a little way back from the street. Their fences supported straggling jasmine that scented the night, and I was full of calm happiness, content to be walking my sleeping baby and my dog.

I came to the street whose name Lawson had scrawled for me, a pot-holed lane of timber houses. The only thing the houses had in common was an immense shabbiness; it was the sort of place where a rainbow flag is used in place of a curtain, where there are several empty plots of land with kikuyu grass as tall as your shoulder and nasturtiums running wild. The narrow roadway was lined with ancient cars and derelict kombi vans. Across the way, appearing like a vision through one of the vacant lots, the skating rink blared an aureole of light and tinny music. It was an ugly place, a beautiful place, and one day a poet might well write a suite of lyrical poems to it. The title could be *Wotherspoon Street*, for that is its name.

Towards the end of the street, music drifted from the back yard of a tall timber house. The space beneath it was filled in with an assortment of old windows and doors, making additional living space. A cluster of garbage bins stood at the entrance, along with lush outgrowths of tropical plants. As I arrived, a car pulled up in front of me. The driver's door opened and someone deposited a pair of silver, laced, extremely high platform shoes onto the roadway. Bare feet were wriggled into them, and the owner of the shoes tottered down the drive.

I took myself, in my flat, shabby brown shoes (for I can never manage to buy a pair of shoes I really care for), with my sleeping baby and my dog, down the side of the house. In the yard, a few people were dancing in a desultory way, but most were standing about under trees hung with fairy lights, drinking and talking. I saw a boy pause in the middle of a conversation to look at me with interest.

I knew that wolfish look. There are certain men, good-looking, confident and predatory, who specialise in it. The boy detached himself from the group he was with and came over to me. 'You look lost,' he said.

'I'm not,' I told him briskly. 'I'm just wondering where to find Lawson.'

'Oh, Lawson,' he said, with a knowing smile. 'He could be anywhere.'

'Then I think I'll go and find him.'

I went exploring. The party seemed to be taking place not just in one house, but in several. Their common yards had no fences, and all the surrounding houses were also lit up, their gardens festooned with lights. There seemed to be no one there that I knew, and I liked that. Going to a foreign country must be that way. You wonder what the customs will be like, and whom you will meet.

A girl wearing pink cut-off slacks with a broad band of lace at the cuffs stopped and leaned into the pram, her breasts spilling out of a skimpy top. 'Oh, how sweet.'

Hetty opened her eyes in a drunken, drowsy way and then shut them again, as though against her will. 'Oh,' whispered the girl, with a finger to her lips. 'I'd better not wake her. She *is* a girl, isn't she?' When I nodded, she smiled and said, 'I thought so.'

'Do you know where Lawson is?' I asked.

'Oh yeah...over in Becky's room.' She gestured.

I went in the direction she'd indicated. At the back of the garden, under trees, was a timber shed with a broad front door standing open. It was lit up inside, and I could see Lawson and Becky Sharp reclining on a big bed that filled almost the entire room. The bed faced the door, and they were lying there not talking, each with their legs straight out and their ankles crossed.

I wondered whether I ought to interrupt, but they were in full view of anyone who cared to pass by. But before I even got to the door, Becky Sharp noticed me and raised her hand in a gesture of recognition. She patted the bed beside her and smiled, indicating that I should join them.

I parked Hetty at the foot of the bed. Tess went immediately to Lawson and put her paws up on the bed next to him. 'Hey, Tess,' he said, rubbing her ears vigorously. I perched next to

Becky Sharp and, after a moment, lay back against the pillows. We all lay with our ankles crossed, staring out at the dark garden. Like people sitting looking at the sea, we seemed to have no essential need to talk to each other. Eventually Becky said, tilting her chin towards the pram, 'She's good isn't she?'

'When she's asleep,' I replied. 'Sometimes she has so much energy I can't stand it. You have *no idea*. It's getting worse as she gets older.'

It was all so easy and companionable, as though I'd known them for years. I looked around Becky's room. It was painted yellow with blue trims, clean-looking and pleasing. There was no decoration on the walls at all. But everywhere, on a desk, on a small dressing table and on whatever floor space there was, were untidy piles of CDs. On a shelf next to the bed, with the CDs, were a few books.

Then someone arrived, wanting Lawson for something. Tess trotted out after him, and that left Becky and me sitting there together, staring out at the garden. The lights and music through the trees were enchanting, and I felt I could spend the whole evening there, just sitting and looking.

'I'm glad you came,' she said. She took hold of my hand and held it lightly, turning it over and looking at it in a detached way. As I'd noticed the first time I met her, her hands were slim and pale, with long fingers. She was like a carving of something stripped down to its essence. I glanced across at her smooth cheek, but she didn't look into my face, just kept examining my hand as if it was a thing of mild interest, a leaf, say, or a stone.

I was happy, sitting there, with my hand in hers. Nothing else mattered. I felt that I was somehow at the centre of the world.

'I thought you said you didn't read,' I said to her, indicating the books.

'Yeah, well ...' she said with a smile. 'It's impossible to have *no* books, isn't it? But they're only poetry. So slender they hardly count.'

I moved over and sat on the edge of the bed so that I could better look at her books. Ginsberg, Ferlinghetti, Corso. William Carlos Williams. Denise Levertov. On her desk was the little case she'd carried that first day.

'May I?' I asked, reaching for it. It contained a silver flute, disassembled.

Just then, someone came to fetch her; the musicians were about to start. Becky Sharp took the case from me and snapped the latches shut. Reaching up to a peg, she took down a beret, placed it at a rakish angle on her head, waved at me, and departed.

———

In fact, as I knew from experience, musicians 'about to start' take a very long time to get going. Wheeling the pram with Hetty still asleep, I wandered out into the garden and sat on the grass, watching them setting up in a space under a large tree. Becky Sharp moved about, setting up mics and amps, testing levels, kicking leads out of the way, and pushing hair away from her face in the inimitable way of musicians, as though she had all the time in the world.

At the edge of my vision I saw Maggie Tulliver. I turned my head to look at her, and our eyes met for a moment and then I looked away. Neither of us made any attempt to approach the other. I wished she wasn't there; it spoiled the evening for me somewhat, but I was determined to ignore her.

Hetty woke up, and I sat with her on my knee. She became mesmerised by the lights and movement. Various people came up and introduced themselves, taking Hetty by the fingers and cooing at her. She was perfectly happy to be cooed at, and greeted each arrival regally. The wolfish boy I had met earlier came over to introduce himself, bowing low in front of me in a parody of courtliness.

'Jack Savage,' he said, holding out a hand.

'Sophie O'Flahertie,' I replied. O'Flahertie was one of Oscar Wilde's middle names, and I used it sometimes because I felt more related to him than to Michael O'Farrell, the man my mother had hooked up with, whose name I'd been given.

I couldn't take my eyes from Becky Sharp. She had opened her music case and slotted her flute together. With apparently random notes floating diffidently into the air, the band started to play.

The music gave me great pleasure, but it was watching the musicians together that I liked best. Each of them managed to be in their own world with the music at the same time as being acutely aware of what the others were doing. They communicated with quick smiles and raised eyebrows, entered into playful volleys of sound, and became lost in trancelike reveries. The music, which had begun so uncertainly, gathered strength.

Jack Savage squatted down next to me and asked me to dance, but I declined. For some reason, I didn't much like him, and I was content simply watching the music. He went away, and a bit later I saw him dancing with Maggie Tulliver. But I kept my eyes on Becky Sharp, saw how her mouth pursed just so against the side of her flute, how she stood so relaxed and upright, as though suspended from some invisible point above her.

I was thinking that I ought to go home at the end of the first set when Lawson turned up, trailed by Tess. 'Come and get something to eat,' he said. He led me up the stairs into the kitchen where people thronged round a long table set with food. He found me a plate, and even selected some choice things for me to eat. He didn't take a plate for himself.

We went to his room, where Hetty crawled about on the

floor and ate pieces of quiche that I popped into her mouth whenever she came close. When she'd had enough, she took the food from her mouth and gave it to Tess.

Lawson's room was at the front of the house, and was sparsely furnished, with a bay window. The bed was unmade; it was single, a monk-like bed, with a thin grey blanket and a flat pillow. I saw his camera sitting on a table, but no evidence of his work.

'So where are these photos you took of me?' I asked. Reaching down under the bed, he drew out a large folder and showed me the photos he'd taken of me on the stone lion. They were of my face. Just my face. In one I wore an expression of brooding intensity, my eyes cast downwards. I must have been reading Oscar Wilde's letter to his mother. Another picture had me gazing into the distance (thinking perhaps of the beauty of the laundromat and Dr Dirt of Dunoon?).

Lawson had other photographs, all of faces. He must have taken them in the street without people knowing, because each of their expressions said something they would not have wanted others to see. People always put on a special face for a camera, just as they do when looking into a mirror.

One man's face said, 'You cannot help me.'

Another's said, 'I am alone.'

'What does *my* face say?' I asked Lawson.

He looked at the picture of me reading Oscar Wilde's letter. *'I wish I was somewhere else,'* he said. And then the one of me staring across the road: *'I belong here.'*

He handed them back to me.

Looking at Lawson's own face, I noticed again the grainy quality of his skin, as though someone had rubbed at it with sandpaper. I wanted to reach out and touch it. Impulsively, I leaned over and put out my tongue. It connected with his cheek for a moment. He tasted, as I'd suspected he would, of salt, as though he'd been standing in sea-spray, or wept so much that his skin was impregnated with tears.

One of his eyes flickered, but that was the only reaction he made. Putting away the photographs he said, 'Do you want to walk up to the park?' Hetty had fallen asleep suddenly on the floor, her bottom in the air, and I picked her up and carried her to the pram without her waking. On our way out of the drive I saw Maggie Tulliver again. She was talking to someone, and affected not to notice me.

We walked away from the voices and music, across the road to the park. There was a brick entranceway with iron gates, but you didn't need to use it, as there was no fence. Immense fig trees, their roots making a maze in the bare earth, stood at intervals where a fence might have been. The park curved around a bend in the river; and through the trees I saw that it was diagonally opposite Samarkand, not far as the crow flies. But there were no crows flying that night. All the birds were silent. Within the park, several more spreading fig trees enclosed little areas of darkness and secrecy. Broad sweeps of lawn were lit by moonlight.

We sat in the open, on the grass, and the air was so mild it was like being bathed in the sea on a summer day. We talked, this salty man and I, in a desultory, aimless, pleasing way. I lay down, stretching out my legs and staring at the sky. At some stage I must have fallen asleep, though I don't remember it. I ended up sleeping the entire night in the park.

———

It was laziness that led to my sleeping the night in the park; the laziness of not wanting to make my way home with my baby and my dog; the laziness of not wanting to move, of not wanting the balmy night to end; the laziness of enjoying talking softly to Lawson, speaking of nothing, my favourite kind of conversation. It was the laziness of simply being me, an abandoned, reading girl.

When I woke in the morning, Lawson had gone, and Becky Sharp was asleep next to me. Someone had placed a rug over each of us, and we had pillows under our heads. Hetty was beside me, curled up with her hand inside the front of my dress. Tess was nowhere to be seen.

I wasn't wearing my glasses, so Becky Sharp appeared blurred and indistinct. I scrambled in my bag and found them. Pushing them up onto my nose, I leaned in close to her.

Her breath smelt like lilies. It was sweet and damp and exotic. She had the lightest down on her upper lip. Up close, I was able to examine the perfection of her ears. Having barely any lobes seemed the only way for ears to be. The ears of other people would from now on appear elephantine. As I watched, her eyes opened, and she lay there for a moment as though unseeing. I saw her gathering herself together; it was an almost imperceptible drawing together of her consciousness, this gathering, until her face became one I fully recognised as hers. She looked at me.

'Sophie,' she said.

She said it in a wondering way. She said it in recognition, as though she'd both expected to find me there and feared that she wouldn't. I felt, in some way, that it was the first time my name had ever been spoken, it sounded so new and fresh and untried on her lips. *Sophie.* So soft and sibilant, it was hardly my name at all, but a new language I had yet to discover the vocabulary of.

CHAPTER FOURTEEN

BECKY SHARP'S HAIR stuck out in all directions, but she was flushed and beautiful from sleep. She yawned, and I reached out and picked several dried leaves from her shirt.

Hetty woke up as sore as a boil, and would not be placated. I felt disoriented and a little ashamed to have spent the night in a park with my baby. Anything could have happened to her while I was dead to the world. I was like one of those feckless nineteenth-century women I'd read about, women who were so careless with their babies that they got drunk and tipped them accidentally into the river, or forgot about them and let the pig eat them.

I gathered her things together to take her home, but Lawson and Tess arrived to fetch us for breakfast. He'd made pancakes, and we ate in the kitchen, along with a few sleepy, tow-haired people I was introduced to but whose names I forgot immediately. There were people still sleeping in and around the house in various places.

My little shrew sat on my knee and crammed bits of pancake into her mouth. With food inside her, she became as sociable as could be. 'Hetty!' various people said to her, in greeting. 'Hey,

Hetty!' And she grinned with a full mouth, stretching out to them with her sticky hands.

I had to get back to make breakfast at Samarkand. Becky Sharp offered to drive me, but I said I felt like walking. I needed some time to gather myself together.

When I got back, I found Maggie Tulliver and Lil making the breakfasts together in the kitchen. Lil bustled about saying something about *sixes and sevens*. It was the weekend, and we had a full house. It had been my job to be there in the mornings, and here I was, draggling myself home with baby and dog in tow at all hours.

They both made it clear that I wasn't needed and they were far too busy to have me interrupt. So I went to bed and flagrantly fell asleep for the rest of the morning, leaving Lil to look after Hetty, who was well and truly awake. Later, Lil told me that she needed more help around the house than I was able to give, especially now I was a student. She'd asked Maggie Tulliver to help out in return for her board.

––––––

And so Maggie Tulliver became part of the life at Samarkand. In the past we'd often had girls working there; every one had left as soon as something better came along. But that's all they had been: girls. None of them had been mature women, and none of them had lived with us.

Somehow, Maggie Tulliver gained rights to our kitchen – other guests had only the use of a little hole-in-the-wall room near the guest lounge that contained only a sink, a microwave and an old bar fridge. She cooked late. I sometimes saw her in there as I strolled around the verandah, the single overhead light illuminating her in a dusky halo as she sat at the table, eating and reading.

Two shelves of the cupboard became hers. They were neat and organised. It seemed she ate things called *amaranth* and *quinoa*. There were packets of thin brown buckwheat noodles with Japanese labels; she had a small exclusive-looking bottle of soy sauce. There was miso paste, and organic brown rice, and Tim Tams. Blocks of tofu sitting in containers of water started appearing in the fridge, along with Asian greens.

Now that she had the status of official helper I no longer had to do her room, but earlier on I'd taken the opportunity to look over her things.

Her clothes looked to be carefully chosen from op or vintage shops. She had a short black velvet coat, and a thin green cotton frock that smelt of oranges. A skirt with red and black squares caught my eye, and I held it up in front of the mirror. It would have suited me as much as my skin, but I resisted trying it on. It was tempting to fling one of her scarves round my neck, or slip my feet into a pair of her shoes (we were the same size!), but I didn't.

Everything was old, but all her underwear looked new. Her drawers contained neat piles of lacy knickers and bras. I touched nothing there, but I thought of my own underwear, which over time had attained a greyish tinge and flabby disposition.

She appeared to have no photographs or any other personal possessions at all. There were no books, save a few university texts sitting on the little table that served as a desk. Maggie Tulliver kept mostly to herself, and we saw little of her.

———

Hetty had a special friend at child care, a boy named Tom, who was three. He was the boy I'd seen her happily with on the day I'd run from the lecture, certain that she was miserable and alone and wanting me. Despite their difference in ages, Hetty and Tom clearly thought each other hilarious and interesting and charming.

I'd made a friend, as well. Phoebe, the girl I'd met at the first tutorial, always sat with me in class, and we studied in a carrel next to each other in the library. When I arrived she was nearly always there. I became familiar with the sight of the tender curve of her neck, smooth and pale, her black hair pulled back tight in a ponytail, the way her fingers incessantly rotated her pen as she read. My books made a whispering sound as I slid them onto the timber desk to stake my place.

I loved the library: the hushed, businesslike atmosphere, the occasional 'Thank God I've finished that!' sound of a pen being flung down onto a desk, the shy coughs, the giggled exchanges between friends.

The library was a good place to sleep, as well, and sometimes I'd snuggle down into one of the easy chairs for a quick nap. I also discovered a secluded nook with a long window that let in warm, dappled light. I'd curl up there on the carpet for short, dreamless sleeps.

It was in that nook that I managed to read the whole of *Ulysses*. It was not on the official reading list, but I read it anyway. I had my own copy, which I'd bought second-hand for five dollars. Like the copy that Kate had described, it had had a hard life. The back cover had been ripped off, but the front contained an enchanting photograph of a street in Dublin. Each day I was in the library I managed to steal a bit of time to lie on the floor in that secluded space, and was transported to Dublin on the sixteenth of June, 1904, the single day in which the book is set.

I could see why it had been banned on publication. I lay there in the library and squeezed and squeezed my thighs together when I read Molly Bloom's soliloquy at the end. I don't think that is quite what librarians mean when they expound the pleasures of reading. Or perhaps they do.

———

But most of my time in the library was spent sitting in the carrel next to Phoebe, with piles of books and journals open around me. When I got sick of studying, I'd lean back in my chair and touch her on the elbow, and we'd go downstairs for a break, sitting with our coffee in the shade of a vine outside the library.

Both of us had become mildly obsessed with our work.

The possibility that writing can be female in style. That was the idea I was puzzling over, and I thought I'd never solve it. What, after all, was 'style'? Was it the words chosen, the way of putting them together, or the particular cast of mind behind the piece of writing? All these things, Phoebe told me decisively. And more. Style was inseparable from the writer's personality; it was inevitable.

Then if so, were there particular male and female styles? Were women meant to be more emotional, more sensual, or what? Or was every style different, because every person was different?

Virginia Woolf had said that one shouldn't write as a man *or* a woman, but be woman-manly. I think that would be very difficult. In any case, I thought that James Joyce had come very close to this when he wrote *Ulysses*. His obsession with the body, his wondering whether goddesses had arseholes and the same bodily functions as humans – I had thought these things myself. And that lovely scene where he burns the kidney and cuts away the burnt bits and slings it to the cat – here is the poetry of kitchens indeed. So I hereby proclaim James Joyce to be an honorary woman!

Phoebe was most fascinated by *Jane Eyre*. '*The madwoman in the attic!*' she leaned across to whisper one day, as we sprawled in two easy chairs on the top floor of the library, reading. She tapped the front of her head. 'We all have one. Don't you think that's part of the fascination of that character? And Jane – she's so *angry* – it's what's inside her – the madwoman. It's what's inside all of us – us women, I mean.'

I didn't think that Phoebe, so ordered and beautiful, so sensible and studious, could have a madwoman dwelling in her attic or anywhere else. Though my own madwoman had been well and truly loose on various occasions, and I told her so.

You?' she said, wrinkling her brow. 'But Sophie, you're so considerate and thoughtful. Such a good mother.' She picked a stray hair from my shoulder and examined it before throwing it away. 'But I suppose all of us have things about us that no one could ever guess.'

———

I disliked reading theory, and avoided it as much as possible. I struggled to make meaning of the peculiar convoluted sentences. They left me cold. I wondered how anyone could ever have a theoretical idea for a novel, because it seemed to me that a novel was all immediacy and thrived on the real.

I turned, as I always had, to novels themselves, and the intimacy of the worlds they described, worlds that I could live in for a while, and which somehow, by some alchemy, enriched my own. I used to love the novels of the nineteenth century best, but now I discovered the women writers of the early twentieth century, those decades of war and anxiety. Jean Rhys, Katherine Mansfield and Virginia Woolf became my new companions.

But I needed live companions as well, and that is why, soon after the party, I returned to Wotherspoon Street.

CHAPTER FIFTEEN

IN DAYLIGHT, THE lane had an air of gentle decay as though everything – the wild ginger that exploded in enormous clumps around almost every house, the splintered timber on the walls and window frames, and even the rusty iron roofs – would soon crumble back into the earth.

As I approached Becky and Lawson's place I heard a piping sound, and followed it into the back yard. The sound made fleeting dashes through the trees as though each note chased the one preceding it, then changed into coiling ribbons, and then again into staccato, breathy pulses. It was music that couldn't be tied down.

Becky Sharp sat out under the trees, upright on a wooden stool with a music stand in front of her. Her feet were planted far apart and she wore an air of industry. She might have been in the act of peeling a load of potatoes into a bucket, or shucking oysters, but she was practising on her flute.

I didn't interrupt her, but instead went up the rickety timber stairs at the back to the kitchen, where I found Lawson eating a bowl of muesli, though it was well past lunchtime. He waved a spoon to us in greeting, and then leaned down and put his beaky nose to Tess's face. She licked him, and he righted himself to face me. 'Hey!' he said.

'Hey!' I echoed.

Without another word he got to his feet and put bread into the toaster. While he was rinsing a fat brown teapot under the tap, Becky Sharp came in and pulled out a chair.

What did we talk about that day? I can't remember. Becky Sharp and Lawson were people who often seemed to eschew words. It was enough for them simply to be.

I helped myself to toast and butter, and when Hetty dropped her half slice on the floor, looking down at it with an expression of absolute dismay, Lawson's eyes and mine met in amused complicity. He cut her another piece from his own toast, and retrieved the lost slice to feed to Tess.

But Hetty didn't *want* the new slice of toast: she wanted the old one, the one that Tess had eaten. She pedalled her legs and became a veritable scold, screaming and flinging the new slice onto the floor to the dog in high dudgeon.

Lawson got up and went out, coming back with a camera slung round his neck. 'D'you want to go for a walk, Tess?' he asked; she wagged her tail. 'I can take Hetty too, if you like,' he said, and at the mention of her name Hetty stopped fussing and looked up at him.

Apart from the childcare centre, I had never left Hetty with anyone other than Kate or Lil, let alone allowed her out for a walk. But Lawson seemed to be in tune with her; he had also noticed her expression when she dropped her toast. We had been like two parents in our tender regard for her.

So I agreed, and he strapped her into her pram, and they set off. The camera round his neck had a sturdy cap covering its lens; it was blinkered like a horse, perhaps in case it saw something that startled it, and shied.

And Becky Sharp and I were left alone. The house was curiously devoid of people that day. Apart from Becky Sharp and Lawson, I wasn't sure exactly who lived there.

We went to her room, and I inspected her books of poetry. One was by Rimbaud, but it was all in French. I opened it up and flicked through, regarding her with a raised eyebrow.

'I did French at school,' she told me casually, and I realised I knew hardly anything about Becky Sharp: where she'd grown up, her parents, siblings … nothing at all, actually, apart from that she played the flute.

I flicked through the book and found a poem that I thought I knew. *Roman*, it was called. It was the one that begins, *On n'est pas sérieux, quand on a dix-sept ans.*

'Can you read this one for me?' I said. 'Translate it into English, I mean? I have a translation in a book at home, but I'd like to hear another version.'

'Mine will be a very *rough* translation,' she warned. 'I mean loose, colloquial, literal.' (She was so stern I found it thrilling.) 'Which suits Rimbaud actually,' she added, and I think I know what she meant, that he was the most colloquial of poets.

She took the book from me and surveyed the page for a while before beginning.

'Okay. *Roman*. That translates as 'Romance', or 'Novel'. I think 'Romance' is closer.' She glanced up at me. How deliciously serious she was – her eyebrows were almost meeting with thought. They were lustrous and black, my favourite kind of eyebrows.

She continued, frowning, hesitating and stumbling every so often as she struggled to get the meaning right.

'You're not a serious person when you're seventeen. On a fine evening, who gives a damn about beer or lemonade and rowdy cafés with shining chandeliers?

'You go for a stroll under the green linden trees on the promenade.

'Linden trees smell good on a fine June evening. Sometimes the air is so gentle that you close your eyes. The wind, laden with noise – the town isn't far away – smells of vineyards and of beer.

'Then you notice a tiny rag of dark blue, framed by a little branch, pricked by a single wretched star – which melts, sweetly shivering, small and white ... June evening! Seventeen! You let yourself get drunk. The sap is like champagne, it goes to your head. You're delirious: on your lips you feel a kiss, quivering there like a small animal ...

'Your crazy heart wanders like Robinson Crusoe through novels (I told you this would be literal! – it probably should go something like "Your crazy heart conjures up all the romantic stories you've ever read") when, in the light of a pale street lamp, a charming young lady passes, overshadowed by her father's fearsome stiff collar ...

'And since she finds you extremely ... unsophisticated, as she rapidly walks past in her little boots she turns with a quick, lively movement ... and on your lips cavatinas die away.

'You're in love. Your heart's taken (literally "hired out") until August. You're in love. Your sonnets make her laugh. All your friends flee. You're *really boring to be with*. Then one evening the adored one actually condescends to write to you!

'That evening ... you go back to the shining cafés, you ask for beer or lemonade. You're not a serious person when you're seventeen and when there are green linden trees on the promenade.'

She fell back onto the bed, as though exhausted by the effort of translating. 'There!' she said. 'I'd forgotten how lovely it was. That was my favourite poem when I was sixteen.'

Becky Sharp struck me as extremely…sophisticated, and I liked that. And she wasn't at all boring to be with. I liked everything about her – those amazing ears that I'd have liked to reach out and touch, the fullness of her bottom lip, and her air of self-sufficiency and mystery that promised many happy hours of getting to know her. I could tell that she was a solitary sort of person like myself; I could have spent hours lying there with her not even speaking, because, as I think I may have said, being with her was like being at the centre of the universe.

Without thinking, I reached out and touched the side of her face, and it was most soft and lovely.

She looked at me, and away.

Then she got up. 'Lawson ought to be back soon,' she said, making for the door. I followed her, though I wasn't at all anxious about Hetty.

I followed her out to the street, and we stood at the side of the road, rubbing our toes in the gravel and chatting. But I felt that I'd somehow spoiled something between us.

Then Lawson and Hetty rounded the corner. He stopped the pram in front of some canna lilies and pointed them out to her. He encouraged her to reach out and touch the leaves, and he picked a flower for her to hold. As they proceeded towards us, Hetty waved the flower about like a fan, and when she saw me, urged the pram forward like a horse. I ran up the street to meet her, my own little hoyden, my boisterous girl!

———

That night it was unbearably hot. Lil had long since gone to bed, and the whole house was silent. When I finally got Hetty to sleep, I went down to my place on the back steps. People walked past in the lane. It was one of those nights when it was too hot to sleep and everyone seemed to be wandering the streets. More than anything, I wanted to be one of them.

I heard someone come round the side of the house. It was Maggie Tulliver. As though she'd eavesdropped on my thoughts she stopped near me and said, 'Why don't you go out for a walk? I can listen for the baby if you like.'

I pushed away my hair, which hung in heavy, damp hanks against my neck. I'd vowed not to have anything more to do with her, but this offer was hard to resist.

'Could you?' I asked.

She came with me while I looked in on Hetty and put on some shoes. I tied Tess to the verandah rail, because I wanted to be absolutely alone. Maggie Tulliver leaned over the railing outside my room, watching as I ran down the front steps.

It was such a lovely long run down those two flights, such a feeling of release! Running under the darkened figs, my feet in old brown sandals fluttered like little flags of freedom. I must have hovered above the ground. Slowing down, and walking at a steady pace, I lifted the damp hair from the back of my neck and felt the air on my skin.

I saw Lismore in all its glory on that hot spring night, and was elated and ecstatic. Everything had a heightened sense of the real and yet an air of mystery: the immense, architectural old fig trees, the garish lights in the main street, the people wandering, like me, to divert themselves from the heat. I paused for a while to observe the secrecy of the river. On the other side of the bridge sat the shuttered and silent hotel, with only a few lights in the upper storeys shining out to show that it was inhabited. I was walking, through habit, on my usual circular route.

I came to Wotherspoon Street and turned down it. Voices floated on the night air. It was too hot to sleep, and there was a feeling of life going on all around me, despite the late hour. I wondered whether Lawson or Becky Sharp were still up, and stopped outside their house, but decided against going in. I was having a perfectly delightful time on my own.

I went up to the park and stood for a while looking at the river. It smelt muddy and rich, full of earth and vegetation. As I turned around to go back, I saw two people lying in the moonlight in the middle of a grassed area. I knew, more by their outline and general demeanour than anything else, that it was Lawson and Becky Sharp. Becky lay on her back, propped up by her elbows, and Lawson lay stretched out flat with his head resting on her tummy. They weren't speaking, or doing anything, just lying there with apparent contentment.

I didn't go to them. I didn't want to interrupt anything, to intrude where I might not be wanted. But mostly, I was perfectly happy on my own. I wanted to keep with me that feeling of self-contained solitude.

Walking back down the street, I saw that the one streetlight had a fuzzy golden aureole. And it seemed that above me hovered a mysterious brooding presence, with soft, curved black wings and calm, scented breath. Somewhere, I felt sure, lurked the poet of Wotherspoon Street, observing this small unimportant part of the world and not writing down a thing.

When I got back, Maggie Tulliver was lying on my bed reading a book. She got up as I came in, and departed, waving away my thanks. The bed was still warm from her body. Her perfume pervaded my pillow. Something about her still made me uncomfortable, and I felt that my lovely evening had been bought at a price.

Chapter Sixteen

A SECRET LETTER arrived from Kate, in the bottom of the envelope that contained a birthday card for Hetty. It arrived the day before her birthday, which was in the early hours of the next morning. The letter was written on a single sheet of extra-flimsy paper, folded into a long narrow strip.

It said:

Dear Sophie,

I know I'll be up on the weekend for Hetty's party, but I needed to tell someone this right now. I'd rather you didn't let Lil see it.

It's very early in the morning and I don't feel quite myself. But who else I might be I can't think. It's just after sunrise and I've had so little sleep I feel almost ill.

Do you remember me telling you about that boy, Myles? Well, I ran into him at a party last night and ended up going back to his place. He lives in an old terrace with a couple of people, who didn't happen to be at home.

We listened for hours to some very obscure blues records (yes, actually records) and it got to be very late.

I fended off his attempt to read me some Sylvia Plath, but ended up staying the night there.

In his bed.

We just kissed for a while in a very uninterested way.

Nothing much happened for a long time, but we didn't sleep. Nor did we talk. I felt very hot and furry in that bed (the household had about four cats who seemed to have shed fur everywhere). I should have just got up and gone home, but I was too lazy, and it was too late and dark, and I felt it would have been more embarrassing to go than to stay.

I hadn't been drinking.

Anyway, just before dawn, after a lot of tossing around and not sleeping something did happen. What do I mean by something? In the end, it was just a lot of inept and rather embarrassing fumbling. And then I went home.

But I don't think that, technically, I am still a virgin.

The thing is, I don't think either of us was really attracted to the other.

That's all. Burn this, if you like.

Anyway, I hope the card got there in time for Hetty's birthday. Tell her I have found her a lovely present.

Kate

Of course I wasn't going to burn it; it's the sort of letter that should be kept for posterity and discovered one day in an old box and read by Kate's descendants. I read it again late that night after Hetty was asleep, gulping it down as greedily as I had the first time, but thinking about Marcus all the time. I had thought that I was over him, but in just a few hours it would be the first anniversary of Hetty's birth. I'd told him the date she was born, but felt sure he would not remember it. I expected that we'd never hear from him again.

So much the worse for him! I thought, sticking Kate's letter down the front of my dress and setting off for the kitchen. Anger and anxiety always makes me hungry.

That night Maggie Tulliver was there, which was annoying because I felt like being alone. She had finished eating one of her late dinners; a bowl sat pushed back in the middle of the table. A few string-like threads of brown noodle were draped over the edge. The sink contained a colander and frypan.

She had a bottle of red wine in front of her, and a glass, and looked as though she was working her way through it while reading a small, slim book. I sneaked a peek at the cover. It was haiku by Bashō.

I pretended not to notice she was there, and rummaged in the fridge for my secret stash of chocolate.

'D'you fancy a drink?' she asked.

I thought *Why not?* and fetched a wine glass. Despite my wanting to be alone, her presence that night made our kitchen seem rather exotic; she looked so worldly sitting with her bottle and glass. She wore a pretty felt hat in shades of brown, pulled closely over her head, and had on a pale blue shirt with red Japanese cranes on it.

Wine trickled into my glass as I pulled up a chair. Her hand had beautifully painted nails. They were bright red, of course, the nails of a witch, or an enchantress. When I offered her some chocolate she declined with a weary gesture of her hand. Before I knew it, I had glugged down my wine and she was refilling my glass. We weren't looking at each other. She kept her eyes on her book; every so often she'd snicker to herself.

I sipped wine and crunched chocolate fiercely, sipped and crunched, until I'd eaten almost an entire family-sized block. Scraps of thin silver foil littered the table in front of me.

'Listen to this,' she said, and read out:

Clouds –
a chance to dodge
moon-viewing.

'Can you *imagine* the pain of feeling compelled to admire the moon on *every bloody single clear night*?' said Maggie Tulliver.

She began to giggle, and I joined her, though in fact I found moon-viewing to be a delightful occupation, and had been taking Hetty onto the verandah almost every night to point out the moon to her. Lil had told me that 'moon' was often the first word babies said, and I thought it might encourage her to start talking.

That night Maggie Tulliver and I couldn't stop laughing. We were laughing at nothing; we would have laughed at anything. When one stopped, the other started her up again.

I finished my third glass of wine, and tipped it up and tried to lick the last of it out with my tongue, *à la* Madame Bovary. But my tongue wasn't long enough, and the wine didn't budge, so I dipped my finger into the bottom where the glass was stained red. I love the colour of red wine more than the taste, which makes your mouth pucker. I enjoyed imbibing that luscious colour more than anything.

A drop had fallen onto the table near the bottle, and I watched as Maggie Tulliver put her index finger into it and smeared it thinly over the surface, like a drop of blood on a laboratory slide. She looked up at me flirtatiously and said, 'Do tell me that's a billet-doux I can see next to your bosom.'

'Not at all!' I said briskly. 'It's a letter from my sister.' I fetched it up and threw it onto the table. 'You can read it if you like.' I felt that Maggie Tulliver's worldliness had transferred itself to me. I was so weary and utterly sophisticated I should have been shot.

Maggie Tulliver took the letter and read it without saying a word. When she'd finished, she placed it carefully on the table and said, 'Sometimes I think the most memorable moments with men aren't about sex at all, which can be pretty disappointing.'

And she told me the story of a trip she'd made to Ireland when she was twenty. While she was sitting at the edge of a lake at sunset, a man had come along and sung a song to her, and then just as unaccountably departed. It seemed to me to be one of those magical and poetic episodes that I had always longed to happen to me.

She told the story very simply, without embellishment. It was myself who, in my imagination, filled in the gaps. I saw the last of the daylight on the water, and a single heron flapping its way soundlessly around the shore, its feet occasionally breaking through the glassy surface of the lake.

'That was when I knew that I wanted to learn to sing,' she said. 'But I haven't got round to doing anything about it until now – almost twenty years later.'

I think I fell a little bit in love with her then. At least, I fell under her spell. I'd have liked to reciprocate with a story of my own, but I had none to match it (for where had I been except Lismore, and long ago an ordinary stuccoed block of flats somewhere or other? The mythical land of my birth in my grandfather's house was something I thought was best kept to myself).

Then Lil hobbled into the kitchen. She had started wearing thick elastic stockings to restrain the veins that stood out in her legs and hurt so much. How mottled those legs were, and so old, when I glimpsed them in bed in the mornings. They had become less like legs and more like ancient textured stone, weathered with age.

That night as I sat at the table with Maggie Tulliver, the bottle of red wine in front of us, I was callous. Neither of us

110

thought to ask her to sit down, or offer her a glass (and Lil loved wine).

As she'd come into the room I'd remembered in time about Kate's letter and hastily picked it up and sat on it. Maggie Tulliver laughed when I did that, a single guffaw. I giggled drunkenly as well. Lil looked at us both sharply as though we were excluding her from a private joke, and we were. It felt as though we were conspiring against her, not just because of Kate's secret letter, but simply because she was old and we were young, and we had been drinking and laughing together. At that moment we were two and she was one. She made herself a cup of tea and went out with it.

In one night I had betrayed Kate and Lil, in one fell swoop.

And because I felt so wonderfully warm and companionable with her, I told Maggie Tulliver about the book I'd just finished for the third time: *Shirley*, by Charlotte Brontë. I got up and ran and fetched the book from my room, and read her bits of it, but not my favourite part, where Caroline Helstone finds out that Mrs Pryor is actually her mother. That part was far too sentimental for the likes of Maggie Tulliver. Instead, I read her the witty bits poking fun at the curates, because Maggie Tulliver seemed to be a poking-the-fun-at kind of person.

There is something you must never do: press a book upon someone simply because you love it yourself and you've been drinking a bit too much wine. But that night I put it into her hands and said that she *must* read it.

Then it struck me that I was tired. I had to be up early for the vigil I intended beside Hetty's cot. I wanted to be awake next to her at the exact minute of her birth. So I left my beloved copy of *Shirley* in Maggie Tulliver's hands. When I found it next morning sitting deliberately in the middle of the kitchen table, I knew that I had abandoned it to someone who had not cared for it at all.

CHAPTER SEVENTEEN

HETTY HAD BEEN born in the early hours of the morning, and slept through the anniversary of her own birth. I put on the nightlight to look at her, and remembered how startled and outraged she'd been, coming into the world. I had been unable to take it all in at the time of her birth, but was overwhelmed soon afterwards. She brought out the extremes in me. I remembered how for so long she'd reminded me of Marcus, and made me long for him, but now she was entirely herself.

I'd read almost the whole time I was in labour to distract myself from the pain: Oscar Wilde. My head swam with it. I didn't know whether to laugh or cry. I did both, in turn.

My baby finally arrived in a great slippery rush, so shrill and indignant that I was awed by the little termagant I had produced. She was so red, so wrinkled, so determinedly unattractive. Kate was rendered speechless, but according to Lil, the baby was perfect, '*a perfect little darlin'.*' I named her Anastasia at once; though I feared her character might be too shrewish for such a pretty name. As Kate left in the early hours of the morning, I begged her to bring me back something to read. I wanted something interesting, something new and challenging. I thought that having a baby might begin to rot my brain, but I also, at heart, wanted to take my mind from the enormous task I'd burdened myself with.

But the moment Kate and Lil had gone, I felt a sudden rush of amazement and love. I floated on a sea of pleasure, and it was only much later that I began to feel tired.

Left alone after the drama of birth, she and I were like two seafarers who'd been struck by a hurricane and had washed up on shore together. She lay peacefully next to me, her tempestuous arrival forgotten. Both of us bore marks of the birth. My stomach, so recently distended, was like a deflated balloon, flabby and wobbly. My nipples were dark brown instead of the usual pink, and there was a brown line of pigmentation from my navel to my pubic hair. The baby had dark hair in strange places (like the tops of her ears) and was pimpled and mottled. In those first days, we were like two impossibly primitive beings. The umbilical cord was gone but it was as though it still connected us.

Before, I used to imagine my life as a car, speeding along a freeway. And I was hanging out the window, the handle of an open suitcase in my hand, spilling out the contents.

And there it all went, whipped away by the wind, almost everything strewn over the road in a reckless extravagance of losing. First of all, to get into the swing of it, I'd lost the big things, Paradise and my grandfather.

Then, in no particular order or importance, I'd lost that little sun-dress I loved when I was seven, numerous single socks, uncountable school jumpers, my mother, the man I called my father, my favourite red silky knickers, Kate's copy of *Madeleine* (plus countless other books she claimed I had caused to vanish into thin air), my virginity (finally! at fifteen), Lil's zebra-striped umbrella ... all of it had flashed past, dropped onto the road, and been lost, abandoned – forgotten, most of it.

But as fast as I was losing I was gaining; the future was rushing up to meet me. I had lost both my parents but gained Lil. I'd met Marcus and lost him. And somehow, I had gained a kind of physical beauty. For most of my life I had been very plain, but since becoming pregnant had become quite astonishingly beautiful.

And then I had Anastasia, who, as it turned out, gained and lost that name within six weeks, and became Hetty.

If I ever needed reminding that I had a body, then having a baby did that for me. I didn't stop leaking blood, and then a few days later there was milk, and tears soon followed.

It was just hormones, all the other new mothers in the ward assured me. It was perfectly all right to cry. Look at them, they said, they wept at the drop of a hat, too, and childbirth wasn't even a new experience for them.

I felt so at home with that group of women. They knitted and watched the television, passed sweets around, and talked about their families. I absorbed the delicious details of their lives, and longed for their problems. They simply couldn't get their children to eat green vegetables (and I imagined myself begging and pleading with a wayward child to eat broccoli to no avail). They never had time to clean the kitchen cupboards (*I* wanted to be plagued by filthy cupboards!). They said that it was so relaxing in hospital that they wanted to stay longer. I listened to it all and joined in whenever I could.

They commiserated with me on being on my own with a baby. It must be hard for me, they said.

No, I told them, *No!* I had Lil, and Kate. They'd seen how good Kate was with the baby. I wouldn't be by myself at all.

But I couldn't stop thinking about Marcus. I undressed Hetty and inspected her for any sign of likeness to him. Her eyes, when she gazed at me, seemed completely her own. Was her skin slightly olive, like his? I peered at her and couldn't decide. But overwhelmingly, what I wanted was to show her to him – I owed him at least that. I'd fallen in love with my baby, and I had no doubt that, when faced by the reality of her, he would too. *Look, look what we made together, in the park that day, and in the red-room. Isn't she lovely?*

As I'd instructed, Kate arrived that first afternoon with a book to distract me, but I was beyond distraction. The book was *A Room of One's Own*, by Virginia Woolf. I put it away for later. *Much, much later*, I thought, and turned with relief to the ordinary talk of the women who shared the ward with me. I was made for ordinary things, I decided. At that time, I thought I might never read another book again.

In that short time I'd also discovered something I knew I'd never forget. I knew that love is not *having* something; it is always tinged with anxiety. It is inevitably accompanied by the possibility of loss.

After Hetty was born, I thought a lot about Marcus. He'd inadvertently left a shirt in my room, a grey, short-sleeved undershirt that had captured the scent of his body. While I was pregnant, I had sometimes worn it to bed, and allowed his odour to cling to me. And when I brought Hetty home from the hospital, I would sometimes secretly wrap her in it, so she would learn the scent of her father. Because surely, she had inherited some of that scent herself, and would recognise its familiarity.

I saw him one last time after Hetty was born, when she was just a few months old. There were posters around town advertising The Innocents. Two nights only.

On the first night I dressed in a borrowed dress and borrowed shoes. Only my emotions were my own, though I wasn't even so sure of that. I had only a sense of heightened anticipation, and an obsessive feeling that I had to see him again. I wanted to tell him about Hetty. That was all. That was his right, after all.

No. Enough lying!

I wanted to see him again. A glimpse would be enough. (Liar!)

I wanted to spend the night in his bed. I wanted him to realise that I was the one for him, to meet and get to know Hetty, and love her as much as I did. I'd longed for him all the time I was pregnant. I'd thought about him endlessly like any empty-headed girl with only love on her mind.

————

He saw me sitting there during their first set and came up to me in the interval. I could see him pretending to forget my name for a while before finding it. '... Sophie. You've changed.'

The dress was far more revealing than those I usually wore. It was tight, stretchy, and low-cut. The shoes were high-heeled and strappy; like the dress, they belonged to Carmen and Raffaella, two old schoolfriends who had more glamorous inclinations than I did.

He asked me to wait for him after the gig and I wondered for a moment whether I was too proud.

It turned out that I wasn't.

Before dawn, as I dressed and prepared to go home to feed Hetty (I had expressed milk for Kate to feed her during the night and now I was full to overflowing), he murmured groggily, 'Will I see you again?'

I told him a time we could meet in the park later in the day.

————

'You've changed,' he'd told me in the pub, noticing only the superficial changes in my way of dressing. But in a whole

116

night with me, he'd not noticed how my body had changed: the stretch marks on my stomach, my full breasts. As I made my way home in bare feet (those tippy high-heeled shoes were killers to walk in!), and walked up the steps of Samarkand with them slung from my fingers like the loose woman that I was, all I could think of was Hetty, and how much I longed for her and missed her.

Kate was at the top of the steps, waiting for me. 'You *do* know I have my English exam today?' she said, as I brushed past her, intent on feeding my baby.

As my milk rushed into Hetty's greedy mouth, I knew that more than my body had changed. *I* had changed. I felt self-sufficient and sure of what I wanted to do.

———

On the way to meet him, I slung his old shirt over the side of the bridge without even looking back, and went to the park where I waited with Hetty beside me on a rug.

He was late, and he approached with a look of disbelief and wonder on his face.

'This is Hetty,' I said. 'I thought you should meet your daughter at least once.'

He said, cautiously, 'What do you want from me?'

Once I would have said, *Everything. I want everything.* I love you. I want *you.*

'Nothing,' I said. 'Nothing at all.'

There was a look of relief on his face.

If he'd wanted, I would have let him see her whenever he wanted, with no strings attached. He could have got to know her, let her call him *Dad.* But I wasn't going to ask him to do all that. It was up to him.

He only reached out and stroked her cheek. And soon after, he left us.

CHAPTER EIGHTEEN

I DON'T REMEMBER leaving my grandfather's house. My mother took me away in the night, bundling me into a car that smelt of the cracked plastic seats. I remember waking at dawn, when we took a pee on a grassy headland overlooking the sea, and then the movement of the vehicle, and sleep, overtook me again. From then on it was all impression – dark, smelly rooms in old pubs and meals of chips and sliced bread, nights spent sleeping in the car, and a succession of broken-down rooms, until at last we came to some sort of stability in an old stuccoed block of flats a street or so from a beach. I had learned the magic of words, and this block had a word set in relief on the front, but still to this day I don't know what it was. I imagine it might have been something like Seabreeze, or Seaview (though there was no view of anything), or, more romantically, Casablanca, or Caliente.

————

That was the place where Kate was born.

It must have been during one of those times when Michael O'Farrell wasn't living with us (and he often went away for long periods, always coming back and 'making up' with our mother before pissing off again).

My mother had a friend called Loretta, who lived upstairs. She and my mother would talk and laugh together, Loretta leaning out the window with her cigarette, so the foetus wouldn't take in any smoke. My mother would hold her belly and say that Loretta had given her a stitch, she'd laughed so much. Loretta had no children, and a wardrobe full of fancy clothes. She worked in a bar at night.

One day, with a sense of urgency, my mother asked me to run up to Loretta's flat and fetch her. Then we gathered things together and went to catch a taxi to the hospital. We'd only gone down one flight of stairs when I suddenly needed to pee, so Loretta rushed me back up to our flat, while my mother waited, leaning against the wall.

That is how your life can change in one ordinary moment. You go to have a pee and when you return you have a new baby sister.

We heard my mother cry out while I was sitting there on the loo, my knickers around my ankles. Loretta told me to wait, and ran out. But I tugged my pants up and went after her. Looking down from the landing, I saw Loretta holding a newborn baby in her hands as though she was in the very act of catching her. She exclaimed, 'It's a girl! Maggie, you have another little daughter!'

I still think of the dramatic arrival of Kate, the imperative of her, her suddenness, the pulsing blue-silver cord still connected to her belly. She was quickly wrapped up in a bunny rug from my mother's suitcase, and doors opened and closed all around us with hollow echoes; there were exclamations and hurrying footsteps.

I went to join my mother, and couldn't take my eyes from the baby's face, and nor, I think, could my mother. There was blood all over the steps.

The baby was very calm through all this. She yawned, and shrugged her shoulders with a slow, deliberate movement. Her eyes struggled to stay open. She gave a feeble, protesting cry, thought better of it, and grimaced so that her entire face was encased in multiple folds. I don't think I was half as enchanted by Hetty's arrival as I was by Kate's. Her hair was very damp when she was born, and was plastered darkly to her scalp. It soon proved to be translucent red. Her face was like a pale rose. She would never be ordinary. She was my own, my darling baby, and I took very good care of her, allowing my mother to feed her and change her nappy before continuing to keep watch as she slept and woke and slept again.

My mother named her Kathleen, *Kate*, after her own mother, she said.

———

And here arrived this same sister, grown-up now (or as grown-up as you can be at eighteen), on the last flight to Lismore on Friday afternoon. She strode across the tarmac, her long legs in black trousers, her red hair tossed about by the wind. She was so pleased to see us that she would not look directly at us at first, only turning her face to us at the last moment. It was composed and private, but I could tell that inside, she seethed with the pleasure of being back. She bent down to hug Lil, and took Hetty in her arms and told her how she'd grown. I could see Hetty waver about putting on an excessive show of shyness and decide against it.

It's impossible to talk on the way home in a car; everything sounds banal and anti-climactic, as though you're saving the important things for later. When we got back to Samarkand, Kate got out of the taxi with Hetty still in her arms. She went slowly up the steps, staring at the house towering above her, as though it was something she'd only ever dreamed about and never expected to encounter in real life.

120

At the top of the first flight she met Tess, who stood anxiously wagging her tail. Kate leaned down and patted her. 'We should have got a dog years ago,' she said, before continuing on, with Tess at her heels, to inspect the rest of the house. She walked slowly, looking about as though sizing everything up. I couldn't tell what she was thinking or feeling. I wondered what she'd make of the place after being away for most of the year; this was the first time she'd been back since going to university. I was worried, actually, that it wouldn't pass muster, that with her new city-accustomed eyes Samarkand would turn out to be utterly depressing and ugly and hopelessly passé.

Kate went first to my room, where she set the mobile above Hetty's cot swinging, and bent down to fan through the pile of books next to my bed. Next she went to Lil's, heading to the wardrobe and flinging the doors open. Lil's clothes had always held a special fascination for Kate; she'd always made free with Lil's make-up and perfume as well. 'Is this new?' she said, tugging at a turquoise frock that Lil's friend Mavis had given to her because she'd bought it too big for herself. 'Dreadful shade,' said Lil with a dismissive shudder, as Kate let the frock fall back in among its fellows. We were all following her around on her tour of inspection; she was like royalty.

Finally Kate arrived at her own room, where she relinquished Hetty to Lil, who carried her away for purposes unknown. Kate looked around quickly before meeting my eyes. 'Everything's as wonderful as I remember it,' she said.

We headed off to the kitchen where she went straight to the jar of nuts in the cupboard. Lil came in, bearing Hetty on her hip. The two of them had an air of sailing inextricably together.

Kate bent down and looked into Hetty's face. 'Do you talk yet?' she said. 'Sophie says you won't deign to.'

Hetty pointed imperiously out the window. She had discovered that you could deflect people's queries by pointing at something; anything would do.

'She'll talk when she has something worthwhile to say,' said Lil with grumpy satisfaction. 'Unlike some. I'll put dinner on soon,' she said to Kate, who munched away inexorably on nuts. 'So don't go ruining your appetite.'

———

After dinner, Kate's friend Marjorie turned up; she was down from Brisbane for the weekend.

She had changed. Only last year, at high school, she'd favoured little cotton frocks. Now, she stepped out of her father's black Saab wearing tight leather pants and a crisp white shirt, with her lips blood-red. Her black hair, always short and curly, was clipped close to her scalp in a style so severely smart that Kate and I simultaneously held our breaths in admiration.

Never demonstrative, she put her cool little cheek up for each of us to kiss. Taking Hetty on one hip without comment, as though she'd seen her only the week before, she said, 'There's a cake on the back seat.'

Kate reached into the car and brought out a plate covered by a teatowel. 'There's a jar of cream as well,' said Marjorie, over her shoulder. She led the way up the steps with Hetty in her arms.

In the kitchen, she rummaged in the cupboard for bowl and whisk. I noticed with greed that the cake had apple all over the top, with sugar and cinnamon.

'How's Medicine going?' I asked.

'I've given it up,' she said. 'I'm working in a cake shop in Brisbane now – starting a TAFE course next year. I'm going to be a pastry chef.' She paused. 'My heart wasn't in becoming a doctor.' Slicing into the cake, she said, 'All that blood. And feeding people beautiful things is very satisfying.'

I didn't comment, though I wondered what her father thought of it. He was a surgeon himself, a tall, thin man with a nervously humorous demeanour.

We sat in the kitchen and ate while Hetty walked herself around, hanging on to people's legs and boldly letting go every so often to fling herself across the gap to the next person. She ate something from everyone's plate, until Lil came in to take her away for a bath.

Kate and Marjorie hadn't seen each other since the beginning of the year, so I said goodnight and left them in the kitchen to talk. Lil brought Hetty to my room, as warm and rosy as a peach in her bath towel, and I fed her. Then, while she slept in her cot, I read my favourite bits of *Shirley* until I heard Marjorie's car leave, quite late. There came a knock on the door, and Kate pushed it open.

She came in barefoot, and padded softly around the room with her hands in the back pockets of her trousers. Finally, she perched on the windowsill. Black sky stood out behind her. Hair as red as hers was a perfect foil for the black. And the short cut suited her, even if she had done it herself. Red walls, red hair, black sky. Perfect.

'Marjorie in leather pants,' I said. 'Who'd have thought it?'

'Why do you say that?' said Kate. 'It's exactly what I'd have expected of her. She can't remain Snow White forever, you know.' She ran her fingers through her short hair. 'By the way, we've got plans for Hetty's party. You can leave it all to us.'

'Right-ho. I thought Lil was doing it.'

'We planned it all out with her while we fed her cake.'

A mobile phone rang, and Kate pulled it from her back pocket. She looked at the screen and pushed a few keys, and put it back again.

'Julian,' she said. 'He's on the desk at the motel where I clean. He just wondered if I'd arrived okay.' I raised an eyebrow. 'He's gay,' she added, casually.

'When did you get *that*?' I said, indicating the phone.

'Oh, not long ago. I *rang* you on it and gave you my number, don't you remember?'

Tess, who'd been asleep on the floor, lifted her head and thumped her tail. Kate jumped down to give her a pat, then parted the mosquito net above Hetty's cot to drop a kiss on her forehead. She came and lowered herself onto the bed next to me. There was something about her that made her different from the Kate who'd gone away at the beginning of the year, something more than the superficiality of the short hair and the acquisition of a mobile phone and a new friend called Julian, whom she'd never mentioned. In some obscure and subtle way, she had begun to grow away from us – from me, from Lil, from Lismore, and from Samarkand.

Rolling onto her stomach, Kate hung over the end of the bed and delved among the midden of books that lay heaped on the floor, reading the back cover blurbs and discarding one after the other. Coming up with *The Bay of Noon* (that browned, dry leaf of a book), she sprang to her feet and took off with it. At the doorway she paused. 'Didn't we have a border collie once? You know. *Before*?'

Before, when we lived near the beach, in the stuccoed block of flats. We were happy there. Mostly. Our lives were only marred by the arrival of Michael O'Farrell, who darkened our door from time to time and stayed as long as he thought fit.

Sometimes my mother would walk with us on the beach, with Kate on her hip and me beside her. And the dog, Jess, would run on ahead, stopping when she got too far away from us, doubling back to wait with wagging tail for us to catch up, then shooting on ahead again.

Sometimes. What a wistful word, the most wistful word in the world. But always (always!) our mother would run into the waves with her skirt tucked up into her knickers. She was laughing, always, with Kate on her hip squealing with delight and shifting her plump feet up and away from the splash of water. Jess would bark and dart forward and try to catch the spray in her mouth.

While I ... what did I do?

I suppose I stood on the edge and watched, so that I would eventually be able to write about it.

CHAPTER NINETEEN

WHEN HETTY FELL asleep mid-morning, Kate and Marjorie surrounded her cot with balloons, and so when she woke she knew that it was a special day. She was full of a delighted gravitas that I'd never seen in her before; at age one, she had come a long way from the newborn she'd been a year ago.

I took her onto the verandah, and we looked down to the grassy area in front of the house. The girls had set out two tables, and hung lengths of coloured cloth from the trees like mediaeval banners. At our appearance, the people below raised their glasses and cheered. It was a blue and gold day, fuzzy at the edges.

So who was there, at Hetty's party?

There was Lil, of course, with several of her rowdy friends: Mavis, Norma, Margaret and Bathsheba (not her real name, but if you can't get to age seventy and choose your preferred name, then what hope is there for any of us?).

Phoebe came, and Hetty's friend Tom, and his mother Colleen, whom I barely knew. Colleen and Phoebe sat and soberly compared their experiences at university as mature-age students, and I was pleased to have acquired such sensible and respectable friends. Tom sat next to Hetty's high chair and they amused each other enormously by opening their mouths wide and showing what food they had in there.

Though we rarely kept in touch, my old friends from high school, Carmen and Raffaella, had come down from the Gold Coast for the occasion. They sat and drank wine with abandon, puffing on cigarettes and cracking jokes that only they could understand. Both had had a spray tan and looked as though they were covered with gold dust.

And after a while Lawson turned up. He gave Hetty a kaleidoscope, one that worked with mirrors and transformed whatever you aimed it at into multifaceted jewels. Of course, Hetty didn't yet know how to look through it properly, but she was fascinated by it. After he'd eaten a few sandwiches, Lawson took Tess off for a walk. He returned with his camera and photographed all of us, which made Lil's friends go all girlish and flirtatious with him.

Kate and Marjorie had made food to please everyone: fairy bread, little quiches and cakes, flatbread rolled around camembert and rocket, rice-paper rolls, and sandwiches filled with egg and lettuce or peanut butter. In the midst of it all Maggie Tulliver wandered up the drive, and we invited her to join us; she did so and was pleasant with everyone, but I noticed she left as soon as was decently possible.

Hetty was passed about from one person to another. After a while, getting the hang of this birthday business, she needed no help to unwrap the presents she was given. She knew she was the centre of attention, and was quietly pleased with everything that day.

I only wished that Becky Sharp had come. I'd called in to the house to invite both of them, and only Lawson had been there, but I'd left a note under her door. It surprised me, how disappointed I was.

———

The party ended, as parties do, with the first people saying goodbye and setting off a chain reaction of departures, until finally the only ones left were Kate and Hetty and me. Lil went to the kitchen with her gang of bawdy old women and drank red wine till well after dark. I left them there reminiscing about which of the men in their lives they'd loved the most ('I will never, as long as I live,' Bathsheba said tipsily, and I thought rather insincerely, 'forget Harry'). I noticed Lil took little part in this conversation, confining herself to listening and laughing.

Then they, too, finally left, and we had cheese on toast for dinner, and Hetty fell asleep in my arms. Later, leaving her sleeping in my bed, I walked round the verandah and past the kitchen window to my place on the back steps. Maggie Tulliver was standing at the sink doing her dishes, saying something to Kate. I saw Kate standing there self-consciously, obviously wondering whether to stay or go. I couldn't hear what they said, but Kate laughed. Glancing in on the way past (all this took but an instant; much less time than describing it does), I saw that laugh was tugged from her reluctantly, as though she was being charmed against her will.

———

At about midnight, Maggie Tulliver came onto the verandah below and sang, just for a little while. I could swear she did it to wake me. I heard her turn on her heel and walk away. Then Kate came from her room and down the stairs (what a restless household we were!). Hetty woke and fussed, but wasn't really hungry and fell asleep at my breast. I rolled her into her carry-cloth and slung her from my front (she was a small child, quite petite, unlike my own strapping self), and went out as well.

Kate was sitting in her fig tree near the river; I saw only the dark outline of her back. I went and stood beside the tree, looking down into the water.

'That woman who calls herself Maggie Tulliver,' she said. 'I don't like her. She looked at me as though she knew something about me.'

I didn't reply.

'You didn't tell her anything about me?'

'Of course not.'

128

The water was black. I turned and took Hetty back to bed. On Sunday, her last full day with us, Kate spent the morning dying Lil's hair; she coloured the front part magenta for a change – Lil loved the effect, and kept prancing around showing it off. Then Kate bathed Hetty, and she and Marjorie lay about for ages in the hammocks talking in secretive voices. 'I miss Alex,' I heard her confide.

She mooched about, ate biscuits, examined her haircut in the bathroom mirror and snipped off a bit more. An old suitcase was packed with books to take back. She and I played Scrabble and she won.

Late that night I lay in bed and listened to all the sounds of the house.

Inside Lil's wardrobe, one of the moths fluttered, and settled itself again. A hair belonging to Kate fell from the bathroom washbasin onto the floor. Lil dreamed and ground her teeth. Kate rolled over and put her arms above her head, her hands making soft cotton fists, just the way she had when she was a baby. In the dining room the breeze rustled the Sunday paper left near the windowsill.

Kate had given Hetty an illustrated book of nursery rhymes for her birthday, a reproduction of an old book. *Lavender's Blue*, it was called. There was one rhyme that stayed with me:

> *How many miles to Babylon?*
> *Three score and ten.*
> *Can you get there by candlelight?*
> *Yes, and back again.*

I liked the elegiac tone, which spoke of loss and regret. And it must be no accident that the number of miles to Babylon equalled the years of a human life.

CHAPTER TWENTY

KATE'S PLANE LEFT at six on Monday morning. We went to the airport in a taxi, and passed from charcoal dawn into the artificial glare of the terminal. And it was there that Hetty said her first word. 'Moon,' she said distinctly, pointing to one of the hideous overhead lights. 'Moon.' We were delighted, though I would have preferred that she'd said it one night as I showed her the real moon. But Kate said that it was good; her naming the light as the moon indicated a metaphorical and poetic cast of mind.

We had a coffee while we waited, and then Kate was gone, swallowed by the plane, which soon afterwards headed off into the sky like a questing bird. Hetty clapped, and Lil wiped away several tears. We went to find a taxi to take us home.

———

I have never had a genius for friendship. I think this is because I didn't grow up in a family where you had to fight for your position. Lil and Kate always loved me unconditionally, and as a result I lack whatever it is I need to shield myself from disappointment. I am too easily hurt; any rebuff causes me to curl up into a soft, vulnerable heap and not attempt intimacy again. But I told myself that despite my deficiencies, Phoebe had come to Hetty's party, and Tom and his mother, too. And Lawson. I'd been at university only a couple of months and I had friends! Friendship didn't have to be this big deal, this all-or-nothing thing, full of drama and intensity.

So when I encountered Maggie Tulliver in the kitchen early one warm Saturday afternoon and she offered me a beer, I accepted. We went out on the back steps to drink, where the afternoon sun filtered through the trees, and sat on the bottom few steps so Hetty could crawl about on the ground.

We sipped beer and basked. When she put down her bottle and said, 'Another one?' I nodded. Screwing off the cap, I sighed with pleasure: 'Beer!'

Hetty pointed to the bottle. 'Beer!' she said, as clearly as anything. Her second word. Maggie Tulliver and I laughed.

'Hey,' she said, lazily, after a while. 'We're doing a gig next Friday night at the uni bar. Just a few of the people from the course. I'd *love* you to come.'

She said it so warmly that I felt flattered.

'Sure,' I said.

We had a third beer, and then I took Hetty to my room for a feed and a nap. Before she fell asleep, Hetty looked up at me and said again, 'Beer.'

We both fell asleep in the sun. I dreamed that she and I were living in a flat-roofed adobe house with a spiral mud-brick staircase going up inside it. In the dream, she could walk, and had blonde hair, not black; despite these differences, she was still Hetty. I took her by the hand and led her up the stairs to the sunny rooftop to take in the washing, and I was very happy.

When I woke, it was still the afternoon and we were still warmed by the sun. I remembered I had to bring the washing

131

in, and while she slept I ran out and did so. And I was still very happy.

————

Spring was rushing headlong into summer the way it does on the north coast. At the university, everything exuded sex – the flowers, the people, the very air. To merely walk about the campus was to be bombarded with stray sexy pheromones. I watched all the younger, first-year students in my classes and felt impossibly old, as though all that flirting and flaunting was behind me. But not quite.

I went to the doctor for a pap smear. The sample swabbed from my cervix was like the string of an instrument being plucked deep inside me; it was a slight, almost erotic twinge of pain.

I asked the doctor about contraceptives, explaining that I wasn't sexually active at the moment but felt that I might be quite soon (this was pure wishful thinking), and he gave me a prescription for the pill.

Bowling across the road outside with Hetty on my hip and the fold-up pram slung over one arm, I came face to face with Becky Sharp strolling out of the op shop on the other side of the street. I hadn't seen her for a long time. As though she'd been speaking to me only an hour before she said, 'I've bought a shirt. For a dollar.' And she showed me a rather boring white shirt with black pinstripes.

We went to the Winsome for a drink, and sat out on the side verandah that had metal bars all the way to the roof, like a jail. Shrubs with red flowers pressed through the bars; beyond them you could see the bridge and the roundabout. I loved it there at once, and knew that it was because I was with her.

'Hetty has a new word,' I told her, and Hetty obliged.

'Beer!' she said, echoing me, and showed a keen interest in taking a sip of it as well. I went inside and got her a small glass of orange juice and she drank that, sipping from the glass with cautious solemnity while I held it up for her.

Becky said, 'I don't think I've ever heard her say a word before. What are the others she knows?'

'There's only one other. Moon.'

'Moon?' said Hetty, peering hopefully at the sky. I loved her innocent enthusiasm for things. Every moment of her life was enormously important for her.

Becky leaned forward and took a sip of her beer from where it sat brimming over on the table, licking her lips afterwards. 'If she learns a few more words she might come out with an interesting sentence one day.'

We made up silly sentences containing the words *beer* and *moon* for a while. Then we speculated on whether this fascination with the word *beer* was a portent for Hetty's future interests. I posited a young adulthood for her spent drinking with friends on the footpath, the way I had done sometimes with Carmen and Raffaella (not outside Samarkand, of course, Lil was stricter than that, but their parents had been hippies).

'I drank on footpaths, too,' said Becky, 'until I read that writing advice from Jack Kerouac. "Try never get drunk outside yr own house."'

'So what did you do?'

'Drank in the back yard.'

I didn't want to leave Becky Sharp that day. After the beer we went and had a coffee at the Dancing Goanna, just down the road, and then we wandered up the lane past her house and into the park. I can't remember what we said. No, I could remember everything, if I tried, but I can't imagine anyone else would find any of it the least interesting.

It started to get dark, and I was hoping she'd invite me in for a while, but she said, 'Maybe I'd better give you a lift home.'

133

'I don't need to rush,' I said. 'We could keep talking.'

She looked past me, her face expressionless. 'I'll get the car keys,' she said.

———

I don't know why I go to pubs and parties because I almost always dislike them. There's too much mingling with people involved, too many occasions to be left out on a limb with no one to talk to, too many opportunities to compare myself unfavourably with others. As the Stoic philosopher Seneca said, you never come away from a crowd a better person. But knowing all this, I went along to Maggie Tulliver's gig, because I'd been flattered that she said she'd *love me to come.*

Whenever I went out I always took a book for company; at the very least I could pretend to be engrossed with that. And it turned out that night that I needed a book (it was *Novel on Yellow Paper,* by Stevie Smith).

I asked Lil to look after Hetty, and arrived not too early, not too late. And I may as well say this straight off: Maggie Tulliver ignored me!

She didn't even acknowledge I was there, though I was sure she'd seen me. I was on the verge of going forward to say hello to her at one stage, but she veered away and spoke to someone else. So I bought a glass of wine and began to read.

Novel on Yellow Paper has a rather loquacious heroine with the unlikely name of Pompey Casmilus. *I am typing this book on yellow paper. It is very yellow paper, and it is very yellow paper because often sometimes I am typing it in my room at my office ...*

The live music hadn't started yet and I felt very conspicuous, and wished I was reading at home in my bed.

... And that is why I type yellow typing for my own pleasure ...

I ploughed on, pretending to be absorbed, and not wanting to leave, as I knew Maggie Tulliver would see me go, and I wanted to hold onto some kind of stubborn pride.

At last the music started, and she sang some sort of scatting jazz thing, and then, no doubt to show how versatile she was, she sang a folksong from hundreds of years ago, which she explained came from the 'cruel mother' series of ballads. It was about a woman sitting near a stream with her baby and taking out her snow-white breast to feed it, and then later slitting its throat with a little knife. I think there were images of blood splashing into the water or perhaps I imagined it.

As she sang I watched people come and go. Becky Sharp came in, with a girl I'd never seen before, a red-haired girl with pale skin and pink cheeks, plump and pretty, but Becky Sharp didn't see me, even though I tried to wave. She and the girl sat at a table and drank beer and looked rather annoyed with each other, and didn't speak much. And then Lawson came in, dressed in an overcoat, even though the night was rather warm, and I waved to him too, but he also didn't see me. Perhaps I was invisible that night.

He looked around and went across to Becky, who spoke to him without smiling, and he wandered away from her again. Then I saw him leave a bit later, looking rather distressed, and Becky got up to follow him without saying a word to the girl she was with, who waited a moment or two before going out herself.

And I sat there all the time with Pompey Casmilus, who was fairly entertaining, after all, though perhaps not as entertaining as all this coming and going, which was rather distracting. *I am a forward-looking girl and don't stay where I am. 'Left right, Be bright,' as I said in my poem. That's on days when I am one big bounce, and have to go careful then not to be a nuisance.*

I looked up from Pompey Casmilus to find that I wasn't invisible after all. The boy I'd met at Lawson's party, the one named Jack Savage, had spotted me, and was coming towards me with an expression on his face that said he was an attractive, irresistible man and that he'd chosen me to give his attention to. The trouble was, in many ways he *was* an attractive, irresistible man, and I was pleased that it looked as though I would have a man and not just a novel on yellow paper to keep me company that night.

'What are you drinking?' he said, noticing my empty glass.

'Wine,' I said promptly, because after all, I am a struggling single mother and not averse to people buying me drinks.

He got us both a drink and sat down and had a squint at my book. '*Novel on Yellow Paper*,' he said. Why do people always read the title of books out loud as though I didn't know what I was reading? – but at least he didn't ask me what it was like, or about. He just sat and tapped his feet and listened to the music. I didn't feel I could keep on reading Pompey since he was sitting there and I was downing a wine he'd bought for me, so we just looked at each other. After a little while he leaned over to me and said, above the music, 'Hey, are you tired of this? Want to go somewhere else?'

I was, and I did, and we drained our glasses and got to our feet. At the door I turned round and saw with satisfaction that Maggie Tulliver *had* seen me after all. I gave her a dismissive glance, and took Jack Savage's arm.

––––––

The *somewhere else* ended up being his place, which was an old industrial shed divided up by partitions, which he shared with several others. I'd not even known what Jack Savage did, but that night I assumed he was a painter (or at least, a visual arts student), as several dreadful canvases in various stages of being

136

painted on were propped about the place. But he may also have been a guitarist, because a guitar sat on a stand in a corner. In another corner was the bed; it was unmade, and occupied by two long-haired cats who looked at us wild-eyed as we entered, and ran off. The bedside table had some make-up on it, which could have meant *girlfriend*, or it may have been his. On the floor was a plate with some dried-out lentils and rice.

But he was fastidious in some ways; an old ironing-board and iron stood ready for use, and a rail had many rather attractive shirts hung on it. The jeans he wore, I guessed, were the only pair he owned. They were obviously very expensive, but filthy, which is the only way to wear ridiculously overpriced jeans. I don't go in for that kind of thing myself.

I put my bag and book on the ironing board. Jack Savage went out to some shared kitchen or other and came back with two stubbies of beer. 'Mmm, *beer*!' I said. I couldn't help wishing I was with Becky Sharp so we could share the joke.

We strolled about the large room sipping beer, and I looked at all his paintings and wasn't at all truthful about what I thought of them. I was aware that I was being flirtatious. We didn't touch each other, but there was an atmosphere in the room that said something was about to happen. The paintings against the walls knew it, and the guitar knew it; so did his rack of shirts. Pompey Casmilus knew it, safe inside the pages of the book sitting there on the ironing board, which also knew it. I knew it too, and it was as if the something had somehow been already decided upon. And that thing was that Jack Savage and I would end up having sex, probably quite soon, there on his unmade bed, which also knew it.

And then I came to my senses. I thought that although Jack Savage was very attractive and desirable, I did not want to do that with him. I would rather be home with my baby.

Naturally, part of me wanted to, part of me wanted the comfort of a warm body and, yes, the pleasure of sex. But I didn't really want *him*, not the way I'd wanted Marcus, who, it seemed, would now be my benchmark.

I put down my beer on the ironing board. 'I have to go,' I said.

He looked annoyed, but was far too cool to protest. I picked up my book and my bag and prepared to leave. But I wasn't to get off that lightly. 'You *are* a bitch, aren't you?' he said, as we walked out the door together.

Oscar Wilde appeared beside me, long black coat, gladioli, astrakhan collar and all. It was he who had said, 'To the world I seem, by intention on my part, to be a dilettante and a dandy merely – it is not wise to show one's heart to the world.'

I didn't grace Jack Savage with a reply.

We left together, Oscar and me, in the direction of Samarkand, and Jack Savage in the direction, probably, of the university bar.

CHAPTER TWENTY-ONE

MY MEMORIES OF my grandfather's place had been real, because our mother took us there, not long before we lost her. We went by train, and he picked us up in an old Land Rover, which twisted and turned its way along dirt roads to his house. I had dreamed of the place ever since leaving it, and it was just as I'd remembered. He was the way I'd remembered him too, and not much older. He still lived in Paradise. I played hide-and-seek with him in the garden. The cherry tomatoes were still there, and still ripe, though it was the next generation of black hens that laid eggs for us.

It was there that I first noticed my mother stumbling, holding out her arms to steady herself. She often stayed in bed and let our grandfather look after us. Now it was Kate who rode around on his shoulders. I held his hand.

I know now that our mother was ill.

Late one night, I heard them talking urgently. He was pleading with her to stay. But she took us away a second time, leaving the dog, Jess, with him, as though she knew that very soon she wouldn't be able to look after her.

When I was fifteen, I started looking for his house. I became convinced that he lived in the hills somewhere around Lismore. I watched out for him in the street, and indeed, there were many old hippies who *could* have been him. One day I trailed one of them around the health-food shop until I decided it couldn't possibly be my grandfather; there was just something about him that was wrong. I thought that if I ever did come across him I would know him at once.

I've always been a romantic like that. At fourteen, I'd read *Jane Eyre*; I remembered how Jane had run away from Rochester and then stumbled around starving until she was taken in by kind people who turned out to be her cousins. And then she found out she was an heiress. Her luck could also be mine!

And so I took to hitching out of town, hoping that I'd see a place I'd recognise. In my imagination, I could see myself going up a driveway, and there he'd be.

At that stage, I was a sullen girl; I exuded a dark aura. I wore layers of complicated and ancient clothing found in op shops. I never washed my hair, and was fat and pimpled. Carmen and Raffaella had schooled me in the minutiae of making myself difficult. I seldom spoke to Lil. I growled at Kate, and froze her out. I did almost nothing but read, and was proof positive against all those proselytising teachers and librarians who imagine that reading is a Good Influence. As far as I was concerned, reading was a down and dirty activity. I read *Lolita* with relish. *'Light of my life, fire of my loins, my sin, my soul … Lo-lee-ta!'* The poetry of the sentences made me swoon. But *Jane Eyre* was even filthier. All that imagery, all that she left unsaid. You didn't need a lot of imagination to know what she was *really* writing about.

When I hitched out of town, every car that pulled up was a potential adventure, a possible prelude to my finding my true identity. Many of the people who picked me up were women, worried about me hitching alone. But they asked too many questions about where I was going – I didn't know the answers, so I began to favour lifts with men. My plan was to ride until I found a likely-looking place, and then get out and explore for a bit on foot, hitching another ride further up the valley when I'd drawn another blank.

Over two months of Saturdays, I went up and down most of the steep valleys surrounding Lismore. I walked up driveways that looked as though they might be the right place, only to be disappointed, time and again. I encountered dogs both fierce and friendly, and people the same. And with each disappointment I lost hope until expectation had drained right out of me.

It was on one of those Saturdays that I had my first experience of sex. I blame *Jane Eyre*. I wanted to find out what Charlotte Brontë so studiously avoided mentioning except indirectly through wild weather and tempestuous emotions.

It was with a boy a couple of years older than myself. I've forgotten his name. He had his P-plates, and drove very fast. Down a rocky side road he pulled over, and we did it, right there on the front seat, without too much of a preamble. I felt nothing really, except stickiness and discomfort; in truth, I'd have welcomed a bit of bad weather to liven things up.

———

I gave up searching for my grandfather. It was entirely possible that he hadn't lived around Lismore at all. Long-lost relatives and fortuitous legacies didn't happen in real life, I decided. And I was getting sick of suffering the leers and innuendos of some of the men who picked me up. I was afraid of getting into a situation I couldn't control. I wasn't such a bad girl after all.

But after that, I started going round with boys. I'd meet them down near the riverbank. I got very little pleasure from these encounters; it was then that I started reading *Anna Karenina* afterwards. *Leo Tolstoy 4 eva*, I should have tattooed on my shoulder.

141

So why did I do it? Was it because for at least the duration of sex I felt wanted and beautiful, even if later I almost always felt the exact opposite? I can see now that reading *Anna Karenina* was a way of telling myself that I wasn't *like* that. I wasn't one of *those* girls. See! I read. I read Proper Literature!

———

Boys used to hang round outside the house waiting for me, and Lil finally realised what I was doing, and she came to my room one night. She told me that I was loved and wanted. 'I love you,' she said. 'I don't want you to go damaging yourself.' She said it fiercely, and hugged me close; I could feel her emotion. It flowed between us. There were our two hearts, beating against each other, and her chin, poking uncomfortably into my shoulder. *I love you too*, I thought. I remembered, regretfully, my mother. I didn't want to lose her. For me, she was still the one. Could I love Lil at the same time?

Lil looked me full in the face and said, 'You don't need to run around with those boys. You're worth more than that.'

And I stopped. Just like that. I kept reading *Anna Karenina*, though. It was then that I asked Lil if I could paint my room, which up till then had been a dull, flaking green like most of the walls in the house.

I chose red, bright red, and Lil and Kate helped me coat the walls of my bedroom with the glossy, sticky enamel paint. From then on my room became like a warm, enclosing womb, where I read and dreamed and wrote the beginnings of at least a dozen novels about impossibly beautiful girls living in exotic countries and which rang so false that I abandoned each one almost as soon as I'd started it.

I didn't go with another boy until I met Marcus. *Tell me the story of your life,* he'd said. It hadn't been until then that I realised I had a story to tell.

———

142

Lil had a story, too. Everyone does. But it's only in novels we can know fully another human being. Real life is different. People are lucky if they're even fully known by themselves.

Lil had been an unmarried mother, as I became. I like the term 'unmarried mother'. *Sole parent* has too much of the smell of social workers. Her son had been called Alan (such a nice, unfashionable, boyish name!) and I only met him once. He was away overseas a lot. He was a 'freelance journalist', which has a great air of freedom and gung-ho about it, though I suppose the reality of it is more likely uncertainty and bouts of penury.

When he died Lil seemed inconsolable. For years her grief so coloured the atmosphere of Samarkand that it's a wonder people kept coming. But since so many of the guests carried their own hidden burdens, they possibly failed to notice it. It was such a colourless house with its brown lino, faded green walls, weathered unpainted wood on the verandahs. Even the coloured glass in the windows was dirty and dull. Only Kate gave any life to the place, and I could see how Lil brightened at her presence. I was a different matter: often sullen, difficult, as dun-coloured as the house.

But Samarkand, as gloomy as it was, had been a saving grace for Lil. It allowed her to be independent, and bring up her son, and later on, support us. It had been left to her by an aunt, or a great-aunt, or a friend of an aunt … Anyway, an aunt had come into it somewhere, and thank goodness for her.

'You're worth more than that,' Lil had told me, and that was a new beginning for the *we* of Lil and me. We became more straightforward with each other (slightly), and I was less secretive (somewhat). But it's probably impossible for people to change their basic natures. Lil would have said of us, 'We rub along okay.'

CHAPTER TWENTY-TWO

SO THERE WERE Lil and I, rubbing along okay in the kitchen one Saturday night. It was about a week since Maggie Tulliver's gig. She had made herself wondrous scarce in that time, and Lil wondered did she still live there at all, though she was somehow always on hand to do the breakfasts.

Lil was making one of her famous stews, with lamb, potatoes, carrots and barley, and sloshing a bit of red wine into it, while she drank the rest of the bottle. It was a kind of Irish stew, I suppose, a homage to the Irish in us, though Lil's surname was Ventura, surely an Italian name if ever there was one. In any case they were two cultures devoted to drink.

Hetty was very tired and grizzly; she had a runny nose and ground her teeth angrily in between chomping on some lamb's liver that I'd cooked for her. I could tell she wouldn't stay awake long enough for the stew.

Someone knocked at the front door and Lil went out. I was expecting it would be someone wanting to book in for the night, but I heard a voice from the hall: 'Is Sophie here?'

Lil arrived back with Becky Sharp, and I was very pleased and surprised. I pulled her out a chair, got her a glass of wine, and she sat there with one elbow on the table, looking around her. I became overly conscious of the Dickensian nature of our kitchen: the crepuscular light, the cracked paint, the filthy old table, and Lil cooking away with cigarette in one hand and wine glass in the other. Hetty gnawed on the unsavoury-looking piece of meat, her nose running snot down to her upper lip; I wore a shabby dress stained with mashed pumpkin, with that morning's porridge dried out on the bodice. You could have mistaken the place for a very low-class orphans' home.

'I'm sorry. I seem to have caught you at dinnertime,' she said. I could tell that she had been very well brought up (though not perhaps well brought up enough not to call round at dinnertime, but who is to know these days when people might take it upon themselves to begin eating?).

'Not at all,' I said. 'People come and go here all the time. Anyway, dinner will be ages.' Hetty finished chewing on her mouthful of liver, and spat it out, grey and desiccated, onto the tray of the high chair.

Becky Sharp said, 'I came to see if you'd like to come out for something to eat. But ... '

I looked at Lil. 'Go ahead,' she said, stirring the pot like a modern incarnation of one of Macbeth's witches (cigarette in mouth to leave her hand free). 'This will keep, and if you get Hetty to sleep first, I'll listen out for her.'

Becky Sharp stayed in the kitchen with Lil while I put Hetty to sleep. It took ages, lying with her on my bed. I was impatient to be away. Once she was asleep, I put her into her cot, found a slightly cleaner dress on the floor, and ran a brush through my hair. In the mirror, lit only by the dim light from my bedlamp, I looked rather scary, all big hair and large, expectant eyes framed by glasses. And also very eager and impatient. I threw a thin shawl around my shoulders and slipped quietly from the room, leaving the nightlight on in case Hetty should wake.

Becky Sharp followed as I ran down the stairs barefoot; I hadn't bothered with shoes – it was a warm night, and I like the feel of the ground beneath my feet. At the same time, I felt that I was flying. Becky and I wrenched our respective doors open at the same time, and grinned at each other over the top of her car.

This was only the third time I'd been in it, and it had lost none of its appeal. So original, so old, but with a CD player which she had installed. You have to have music while you're driving. For a while we just drove around, and ended up at the lookout on Girard's Hill. 'What do you feel like eating?' Becky asked. Lismore lay below, lights strung along the main roads, the city centre shining feebly, and house lights dotted between trees. Night and distance made the place look larger, with more possibilities.

'I'm not very hungry.'

'Me either.'

So we decided on takeaway falafel rolls. We parked downtown near the shop, and sat looking for a while at the people wandering about. Up close, Lismore is not the most exciting place to be on a Saturday night (or, indeed, many would argue, at any other time). There was a choice of several pubs, with or without live music, a nightclub (actually also in a pub), various takeaway food places, a couple of restaurants … but people were out and about, anyway. 'Look at them,' said Becky. 'All of them looking for *the heart of Saturday night*.'

'Oh!' I said, breathless. 'Do you like Tom Waits?'

She said, at the same time as me: 'I *love* him,' both of us with such fervour that we burst out laughing.

She put Tom Waits on, and we drove down to the river and got out of the car to eat, leaning against the bonnet.

'I like Lil,' she said. 'Lawson told me about her, but I didn't believe she was just as he said.'

'I *love* her,' I said, imitating the way I'd spoken about Tom Waits. And it was true, I did, though I don't think I'd ever told her that.

I wanted to know more about Becky Sharp. Up to now, I'd known very little about her. She said that she'd come up from Sydney to go to university three years ago. The School of Contemporary Music seemed an obvious choice. Her parents had wanted her to stay in Sydney and do law, but she'd been interested in music all her life, and while she was still at school she'd started using the instrument they'd chosen for her to learn – the flute – in rock-type arrangements.

'I like living here,' she'd said. 'Everyone at school (it was a posh girls' school) was going to uni in Sydney, and I wanted to get away from all that.'

'All what?'

'Knowing everyone. Being part of the crowd. They'll all end up marrying lawyers or fancy restaurateurs – some of them are engaged already.'

She flicked sauce from her fingers disdainfully, as though flicking away her past, and then licked them clean.

'And Lawson?' I asked, thinking of their apparent closeness. 'Are you and he on with each other or anything?'

Becky laughed so much that she started coughing. 'No,' she said, shaking her head. 'No. Nothing like that. We're just housemates and friends. Actually, Lawson thrives on unrequited love. I think he'd run away if anyone ever reciprocated it. I think maybe the only thing he really loves is photography.'

'Who does he have unrequited love for?'

'Jack Savage, at the moment.'

'Oh.'

'Do you know him? Bad choice, was my advice about him. Even if he was gay, Lawson'd do well to stay away from him. Now, tell me about you.'

So I told her. I told her everything that I'd told Marcus that time, and more, because I told her about him as well, and how I'd come to have Hetty. I told her about searching for my grandfather, and the boys on the riverbank. It took a long time, but not, it must be admitted, all night.

And at the end of it all, Becky looked up and said, 'I don't think anyone has ever told me that much about themselves.'

I didn't know what to say to that. Was I odd? Was I *very* odd?

She reached out and touched my arm. 'It must be late,' she said. 'I'd better take you home.'

But I didn't want to go; I was dismayed, but torn as well. I thought of Lil, who even now was probably fussing about in the kitchen warming a bottle with Hetty on her hip.

But Becky Sharp didn't make any move to go. She leaned back against the car. We were very close.

And then, taking my courage in both hands, I leaned forward and kissed her on the mouth. Perhaps it was a way of keeping her there with me.

I remembered the time I'd first tasted an olive. It had been strange and unfamiliar, and I wasn't sure that I liked it. I almost spat it out, but was intrigued, and after a while I knew that I liked olives after all.

It was the same with Becky Sharp's kiss, which wasn't just a kiss, but a chance to see her up really close, touch her beautiful ears with my fingers, and her soft mouth.

'Come back to my place,' she said, and so I did. We went to her room, and she closed the door.

CHAPTER TWENTY-THREE

I WANTED TO STAY in her bed all night, but I had Hetty to think of.

After she dropped me off at home, I waited for her car to go, gathering myself together. There was much to be gathered, because being with Becky Sharp had scattered all my preconceptions of myself. I could hear Hetty wailing up there in the house and yet I still hesitated to go in. I wanted to be by myself to think.

But I was a mother, so I made my way up the front steps to where rooms blazed with light and Hetty screamed fit to wake the dead. There was Lil, jiggling her in the kitchen. Hetty's nose and eyes streamed; she was almost choking with fury and flatly refusing the bottle of milk that Lil offered her.

Maggie Tulliver was in the kitchen too, and gave me a sly, triumphant glance as I appeared, barefoot, wanton, my clothes awry and hair loose, my eyes, no doubt, vacant with bliss. There are times when you know that everyone can see by looking at you exactly what you have been doing.

'She won't settle, poor little motherless mite,' said Lil, followed by, 'Exactly where have you been all this time, madam?' as Hetty flung herself into my arms and her sobs subsided.

'Just … talking with Becky Sharp,' I said.

'Till three in the *morning*?'

'We had … many things to discuss.'

I took Hetty to my room and soothed her to sleep. Then, for what was left of the night, I kept waking and thinking about Becky Sharp. After that first, astonishing kiss, it seemed natural to me that love should be so unclassifiable and surprising. Why should there be rules about whom you could love? I'd always had a mind to flout rules. At the same time, it had begun to come into my mind that if I were to be with Becky Sharp it would change my life in some profound and unalterable way.

I wanted so much to see her again, but was content to wait. I was so happy I went out and squandered an obscene amount of money, on new shoes. They were of soft red leather, ballet flats with a broad leather tie at the ankle. My legs looked lovely in them.

I bought Hetty some shoes as well, because she had started taking her first steps, and she might soon want them for running round town in. Hers were blue. I thought that if we both wore red shoes it would spoil the effect of mine (vain Sophie!). She said her third word: *shoe!* as I wriggled her foot into one. Or was it blue? 'Blue shoe,' I told her, hoping that didn't confuse her too much.

Both of us loved our new shoes. 'New blue shoes!' I told her gleefully. I wanted to dance my shoes to pieces the way the princesses did in that fairy tale, so I took Hetty round to Becky Sharp's place.

But she wasn't there. Lawson looked rather embarrassed to see me.

'She had to go over to Byron Bay,' he told me. 'She said, if I see you, to tell you that she'll catch up with you later.'

He couldn't quite look me in the eye, so I suspected he might be not quite telling me the truth. I was dismayed. I felt that she was avoiding me, and that she might feel that what had happened had all been a mistake. For me, it had been absolutely right.

That day I gave the dog, Tess, to Lawson, because he was her true owner; I felt that she'd been merely in my care. But in giving away the dog so readily, I wondered if I was also anticipating having to give away my love for Becky Sharp.

A couple of days later, while glumly pushing Hetty's pram around the streets, I came across Lawson sitting on a seat next to the footpath. He had his camera slung round his neck, and he and Tess were sharing an apple.

'Hello,' he said, as I sat down beside him. He cut a slice of apple with a pocketknife and offered it to Tess, who took it with a look of devoted resignation; I knew she didn't really like apple. As an afterthought, he cut another slice and gave it to Hetty, who did.

'Is Becky avoiding me?' I said.

Lawson shot me a pained look. 'It's not up to me to tell you what she's doing. But I don't want you to get the wrong impression,' he added quickly. 'She told me she really likes you. She's just spending some time … tying up a few loose ends.'

'I see,' I said. 'That red-headed girl…?'

He nodded. 'Victoria,' he said. 'Her name,' he added, when I looked puzzled. 'It hasn't been going well between them for a long time. On and off again…'

Victoria! I didn't think I wanted to hear. 'Okay,' I said. 'I get the picture.'

I kissed him on his salty cheek and left, stopping at the Winsome on the way home. I got myself a beer and Hetty a juice. We went outside where we'd sat with Becky that time. It now seemed so long ago. I sat down and admired my shoes, a bit sadly this time. Hetty saw me looking and said, 'Shoe!'

'Beer!' she said, and 'Ju.' (Juice. Words were accumulating so fast in her vocabulary she would soon be composing the works of Shakespeare.)

I went and got us some crisps, and we sat outside on the verandah and talked about moons, shoes, juice and beer till almost dark. I thought about Becky Sharp all the time; she hadn't been absent from my mind since that night. Now that I'd had time to digest the information, this *Victoria* didn't bother me too much at all, even though I remembered her as being impossibly lovely with her red hair and white skin. Becky Sharp and I belonged together. I was still a hopeless romantic. I imagined the green frog car coming miraculously over the bridge, and I'd run out and she'd see me, and stop.

But that didn't happen. At last, the moon rose in the evening sky, and we went home.

———

I threw myself into study.

Is it possible for writing to be female in style?

To that end I finished reading *Novel on Yellow Paper*. Pompey Casmilus wasn't the narrator's real name, but she thought of herself as a seedy old Roman emperor type. I knew what she meant, because I feel like that sometimes.

Like many books, it all turned on the question, *Should this woman marry this man?* and the answer in this case was most definitely no, in fact poor Pompey was heartbroken a couple of times. Stevie Smith had lived all her life as a spinster though I read somewhere she'd possibly had an affair with George Orwell, who was married to someone else. In the end, though, I could not describe this book adequately – I will merely say that if you had a mind to, you could become very annoyed and oppressed by her way of putting things.

Then I read *Nightwood*, by Djuna Barnes.

'This book is very strange,' I told Hetty as I hung out the washing. 'Apparently publishers told her that it was not a novel, because there was no continuity in it, only high spots and poetry – she didn't give anyone any idea of what people ate or wore or how they opened and closed doors.' Hetty was my sounding board. When you're involved in academic work, I found, you needed someone to express your ideas to, even if they gave you no feedback whatsoever.

'And in a way they're right – I can't remember anything happening, only images – but what does that matter? It's so strange, I love it, though I doubt I have any sort of grip on it at all. But maybe some things, like poetry, weren't meant to be gripped.'

Hetty's rejoinder to this was to pull herself to her feet at the barricade to the stairs and point to some unseen object. 'Moon,' she said (she saw moons everywhere now). She was dressed that day in red-and-white striped leggings and a purple T-shirt given to her on her birthday by Bathsheba. It had splashes of porridge and orange juice all down the front.

Next I read a short story called 'The Debutante' by Leonora Carrington, which I found in a book called *Wayward Girls and Wicked Women*.

It's quite surreal. A girl doesn't want to go to a ball, so a hyena she meets at the zoo goes to the ball in her stead. It kills the girl's maid and uses her face as a disguise, and ends by saying to its fellow diners, 'Think I smell a bit *strong*, do you?', rips off the face and eats it, and escapes through the window.

All of the books I read, published in the 1920s and '30s, sounded as if the authors were at once furious and curiously happy about being a woman, and that only by very strange writing could they begin to express this. I think women are more peculiar than men. It's what I like about them.

Is it possible for writing to be 'female' in style? I got my essay in on time and was awarded a Credit, not too bad, considering I'd not written anything much since I'd left school. The tutor's comments said, 'Sophie, this is quite original and entertaining but would have been improved by a wider reading and application of theory, rather than relying on your own subjective reactions to novels.'

———

A week later, I'd still not seen Becky Sharp, and to be truthful I'd given up wandering about, hoping to run into her. I had a possibly unfounded feeling that everything would be all right. She had said that night, as I got up to go home, 'I love you in my bed.' Which was almost like saying she loved me, wasn't it? Though in my worse moments, I told myself not to be pathetic, and that girls were probably as bad as boys in saying what they didn't mean after sex.

And for some reason (perhaps because Becky Sharp wasn't the first girl I'd kissed) I thought about Allegra, who had been the first.

———

Allegra and I were the same age: we were nine. She and her mother stayed at Samarkand for what seemed like ages to me, though it was probably weeks rather than months.

I can remember Allegra the first time we encountered each other. 'What's *your* name?' she said. That was the most thrilling thing anyone had ever said to me – 'What's *your* name?' – because it promised so much.

'Sophie,' I told her.

'I'm Allegra.'

Allegra and I became like *that* (imagine two fingers crossed) at once. She was very small and olive-skinned, with curly brown hair. Seldom very clean, she had wonderful clothes: beautiful hot-pink socks, and a fluffy little cardigan in the same colour. She was always hungry, and I was always taking her into the kitchen for food. I think her mother often didn't bother feeding her.

Her mother's name was Natasha; she was tall, with beautiful long legs and olive skin like her daughter. I heard Lil saying one day that she was *no better than she should be.*

Natasha often had men in her room. When she did, Allegra came to me. We slept many nights squashed into my bed. I talked in my sleep and Allegra often woke with night terrors, so we disturbed each other all night. 'I'm so glad I know you,' she'd say, snuggling up to me. Otherwise, I don't know where she'd have gone when her mother had men in her room. Stayed there with them both, I imagine now.

When her mother wasn't entertaining men, Allegra and I used to hang around in their room, eating lollies and trying on her mother's make-up, while Natasha smoked and read books. I was very happy then; I imagined how good it would be if I still lived with my own mother. I missed her desperately, and thought Allegra was so lucky to have a mother. I told her so.

'What happened to your mother?' she asked me.

'She died.'

'How?'

'She got very, very sick, and had to go to hospital and everything.'

I felt momentarily important as I said that, as though it was a very distinguished thing. It was the first time I'd voiced it to anyone.

———

It was down near the river, hidden in the long grass and weeds, where Allegra showed me what her mother and the men did together. She lay on top of me and wriggled around, and panted, and she pressed her mouth onto mine with her lips firmly closed. It felt like someone shoving something into my face, and I said to her, 'You don't do it like that. You do it like this.' And kissed her softly and tenderly, so I could taste the inside of her mouth (it was like raspberry lollies). And I did feel very soft and tender towards her.

But she got to her feet at once and ran away.

It wasn't long after that that she and her mother left. I heard Lil saying to Natasha that she didn't want Samarkand turning into 'a house of ill repute'. Natasha retorted scornfully that the place was falling apart and didn't have much of a reputation anyway.

They left without saying goodbye. In the room they'd occupied was left a clutch of lolly wrappers, an old black bra, a few newspapers, and a book. I later found one of Allegra's socks under my bed, covered in balls of fluff. I threw it in the river.

I kept the book, though, because even at that age I liked collecting books, even if I didn't yet understand them, and that one was incomprehensible. I've just searched it out. It's a book of philosophy by Ludwig Wittgenstein, called *On Certainty*, and inside is scrawled the name Natasha Jones.

I wanted Allegra to live with us forever, and I hated Lil for ages after that.

part two

Chapter One

ALL I CAN think as I write this is that Lil is dead.

She died before I began writing this ... whatever it is that I'm writing. Memoir or novel? It doesn't matter.

I remember months ago, when I began to write. I sluiced my face with water and examined it in the mirror. I had recently lost one of the people that I loved most, and at the same time, I was *in* love. How contradictory life was! The face that looked back at me was little different. And yet inside, how I had changed. I decided to write my story.

Beginning was the hardest thing. I found that the only way was to jump in.

So I lit a candle to gaze at, and sat down. And now I have come this far, and I find that in order to go on, I need to begin again – or at least, I need a change of tempo. I need to come to grips with what comes next.

Well, *No paper ever refused ink*, as the saying goes.

As though writing is merely the running of a pen over a page, which will suck up words as a thirsty woman does water. If only it were so simple!

I would like to be able to say that I'm writing on thick white paper with a beautiful fountain pen in black ink, but I'm doing it on a computer, a very old Mac that was being thrown out in a council clean-up. I came along just as someone was putting it out on their grass verge and said, 'Does that thing still work?'

The man told me that it did, so I plucked Hetty from her pram and gave her to him to hold, and put the computer and all its bits into the pram, and pushed it home triumphantly with Hetty on my hip. And it works perfectly!

Someone once told me that I had a beautiful Irish face, but he was drunk. My name may be O'Farrell, same as Kate's, but that was *her* father's name, not mine. 'Sophie' is my only true name, and is supposed to mean 'wisdom' in Greek. In my dictionary it says 'sophism' is a false argument intended to deceive. Contradictions! But after all, contradictory aphorisms were Oscar Wilde's stock-in-trade.

But I am procrastinating. What I am trying to say, what I am trying not to say, is that Lil is dead.

———

The day she died, I came home from the hospital and the house felt empty. I slept all day. Late that night I went to the kitchen and sat at the table, my face propped against the palm of my hand.

She was all I could think of.

I remembered the way she'd prepare vegetables. Potatoes would be peeled hours before she needed to cook them, and sit dwelling under water in a pot like strange pale creatures from another world. She'd zip the vegetable peeler quickly down the sides of long green beans and then slice them neatly on an angle. They'd spill one after the other into a bowl like green arrows, each exactly alike. And against my advice that all the nourishment was in the skins, she'd flay carrots with swift movements, and slice them into neat rounds.

Then she'd boil the hell out of everything.

Oh, all the old-fashioned, overcooked meals we'd eaten in that kitchen! The room was exactly the same as it had been when I'd arrived in the house, except that the pale green of the walls had faded even more. The coloured glass in the windows made the room feel like a place of worship. Only the worn linoleum had been replaced by newer stuff in an ugly modern design. And Lil had painted the chairs lavender, her favourite colour. She had an old lady's taste in everything.

Her hair was very thin. She always insisted on dying it black. It was soft, like the hair of a baby. She had that old-lady smell, too, for as long as I'd known her.

Lil and I were so alike.

Though it was true that no amount of instruction could teach me to cut beans into that elegant shape, and I was slothful and slatternly in my habits whereas Lil was a powerhouse of efficiency, we were true soul mates. Both of us had been mothers without the benefit of a man around (if, indeed, benefit it be!). Both of us loved cake, and could sit replete in that kitchen together with a cup of tea and crumb-filled plates in front of us for ages. I can't remember what we spoke about. Nothing in particular, which is a sign of the deepest intimacy. And we loved to read. I believe now that it was Lil who made me into a reader, which has been one of the greatest comforts in my life.

———

The night after she died, I stretched my arms out across her kitchen table and fell asleep with my head on the wooden surface.

Being alone in Lil's kitchen was the only thing I wanted to do. I couldn't see what lay ahead of me, or what I would do now.

I only knew that I wanted to live in that house forever, and cook meals in that kitchen, and become an old lady there, with old-lady habits, and an old-lady smell.

———

Life changes so suddenly. If that is a truism, if it's what many people say after a great personal loss, then it's a cliché exactly because it is true.

I came home from my morning walk with Hetty (a fine day – a day that promised to be sublime) to find an ambulance pulling away from Samarkand. Maggie Tulliver, who stood on the verandah watching it leave like some attendant harpy, told me that Lil had collapsed on the kitchen floor.

I called a taxi and went to the hospital, and stayed by Lil's side for almost the rest of her life.

'She's my grandmother,' I told the nurse, and they finally let me in to see her. She was in Intensive Care, unconscious, and hooked up to tubes and monitors.

I went to the public phone and tried to call Kate, but her mobile was switched off.

All day, Lil drifted. I held her hand, hoping for a sign from her. Hetty bounced around on the edge of the bed, crawling up close to put her fingers in Lil's mouth, as she used to do in bed with her in the mornings, until one of the nurses suggested I put her into casual care at the crèche down the road. She howled when I abandoned her there, but the truth was, I didn't have the energy to watch both of them.

In the afternoon, Lil opened her eyes. 'I think I must be dying,' she said to me, her eyes wide.

'No,' I said, putting my hand on her arm, 'the nurses say you're stable now.' That was the truth. *Serious but stable*, I could have said, but it sounded worse.

I'd called Kate again, but still no answer, and no message bank.

Lil slept, and I had to pick Hetty up by six. The nurses told me I should go home for a break and come back later.

So I went home, fed us both, and finally got onto Kate, who rang back later to say that the next plane didn't leave till six the following morning, but that she'd be on it. Kate was in tears, and kept insisting that I tell her *exactly* how Lil was. No lies, she said, knowing how I could tweak the truth.

Serious but stable, I told her. And what was wrong with her? she wanted to know. *Her heart.* Her big heart was giving out.

Then, because Maggie Tulliver offered to babysit, I left Hetty asleep in her cot at Samarkand, and went back to Lil.

———

When I arrived Lil had opened her eyes. She wore an oxygen mask, but she dragged it aside to kiss me hello.

I'd brought some of her nighties, and a dressing gown, which I stowed away in her bedside chest. I put a bottle of lemonade and the grapes I'd brought on top of it.

'Is it night?' she mouthed.

I nodded. 'And Kate will be here in the morning.'

A shadow passed over her face. 'So far for her to come,' she tutted, 'when I'm going to be all right.' A tear ran down her face. I wiped it away.

'Would you like a sip of lemonade?' I asked. She shook her head. 'When I get out of here,' she wheezed, 'I'd love a whole bottle of red. And a big steak.' She smiled. 'Gawd, I could do with a ciggie.' But of course, I'd not brought any, and anyway, she was in full view of the night nurse.

She told me that her friends had been, but only a few had been allowed in. 'I'm glad,' she said. 'Too tired for anyone but family.' She closed her eyes and I thought she'd fallen asleep. I held her hand and watched her slow, laboured breathing.

A pressure on my hand made me lean closer. Without opening her eyes, she said, '... always wanted you both.'

———————

Lil fell asleep, peaceful and composed. The nurse told me that I could go home if I wanted to. She would sleep for ages, and I could come back tomorrow. They'd ring if there was a change.

Anxious that Hetty might have woken and found me gone, I went home. There were lights on, on the verandah, and in the kitchen. I presumed that Maggie Tulliver must be in bed. We had no guests, having turned a couple away that day because Lil was ill.

When I got to my room my nightlight was still on, and Hetty lay awake in her cot. She whimpered when I walked in, and I saw that her eyes were wet. Her face was red; she looked as though she'd been screaming and had at last given up without hope of ever being heard. I never allowed her to do that.

She sat up and almost leapt into my arms, and I fed and changed her. I walked with her down to Maggie Tulliver's room and knocked. There was no one there. We returned to my room; Hetty fell asleep beside me on the bed, but I lay there until I heard footsteps on the stairs. Then I went out, switching on the outside light. Looking down, I saw Maggie Tulliver and Jack Savage, their arms round each other, just arriving at the first-floor landing. Maggie Tulliver stopped, and my eyes held hers with the force of my will. I had not undressed, and gathered my cardigan around me as I descended to where they stood.

'How long have you been out?' I said. 'When I got back Hetty looked as though she'd been screaming the house down.'

'I was only out for a while.' She made to continue on her way, but I took hold of her arm fiercely.

'You offered to look after my baby and you left her alone.'

'She's okay, isn't she?' said Jack Savage. 'House didn't burn down or anything?'

'*You – never – leave – babies – on – their – own! Everyone knows* that!'

I stormed back up the stairs and paced restlessly around my room. I wanted to go to Maggie Tulliver and hit her so hard it would draw blood.

Instead I threw some of Hetty's things into her pram and took it down the steps. Then I lifted my sleeping baby and carried her to her pram. In fury, I strode through the midnight streets. A car crawled beside us for a while, and hooted. I gave it the finger. The streetlights were small universes with circling moths. I crossed the black, oily river; the Winsome Hotel was dark and shuttered.

I walked instinctively and purposefully towards Becky Sharp's place, though I had no idea why, or what I would say when I got there. I simply *needed* her.

The door of her shed was shut, and I knocked urgently and called out. Light was suddenly thrown through the side window onto the bushes outside. The door opened, and she stood there in T-shirt and knickers, frowning and still half asleep, her eyes adjusting to the light.

'Sophie?' she said. 'What's wrong?'

It was only then that I was able to cry. I blurted out something about Lil, and about Maggie Tulliver and Hetty, and I sobbed and sobbed, with her arms around me.

Then I stopped. 'Look, I need to get back to the hospital now.' It suddenly seemed the most urgent thing in the world. 'Can you take me there and then go back to my place with Hetty and look after her?'

It seemed so long ago, the last time I'd ridden in her car,

because I'd not seen her since. It was the night I'd gone to her room. So much had changed since then, but between us, nothing had.

At Samarkand, the lights were on. Maggie Tulliver met me at the top of the stairs. The hospital had rung and wanted me there at once.

———

Whichever way I write it, no matter how many times, the ending is still the same.

Lil died.

Becky Sharp drove me back to the hospital, and then took Hetty (still sleeping, exhausted from crying) back to her cot, and stayed the night with her in my room.

It seemed I didn't need to speak to Lil. When I asked her, silently, in my mind, if it had all been worth it, if *life* had been worth it, all the sorrow and loss, the pain of dying, she opened her eyes for a moment and said, 'I've had a wonderful life. You and Katie, and Alan ...'

A little while later (her bed shielded with curtains, for the privacy of dying) she seemed to be unconscious. I walked, almost in a dream, to the far end of the ward, and saw through the window that it was still night. I had heard that most people die in the night, and had some idea that if she could make it through till dawn she'd be all right for another day. I thought that if I stayed with her I could will her to live.

When I came back, I took her hand and held it, and with her eyes still closed, she put up her mouth for a kiss. I bent down and kissed her tenderly on the lips, the way she had always kissed me when I was a child at bedtime. I had thought then that I was merely taking her kisses and keeping my heart for my mother, but I saw now that that had never been true. How can you take love and not give back?

I kissed her mouth again, and then again, very softly.

Soon her breathing became more laboured. She struggled to say, 'Tell Katie ... '

I knew that she couldn't wait for Kate.

'I know,' I whispered. 'I'll tell her. It's all right. It's all right to go now.'

She died an hour later. By the time the sun came up, she had gone.

CHAPTER TWO

BECKY SHARP MET me in the lobby of the hospital, Hetty on her hip, and it was dawn when the green car pulled up at Samarkand.

Maggie Tulliver was in the hallway. 'I can stay if you like and...'

'I'd rather you went,' I said. 'I'm closing the place up for a while.'

She left in an old car with Jack Savage, as Becky and I were going to the airport to pick up Kate.

The house was very empty when we got back. Kate went at once to Lil's room and I left her there by herself. I wrote on a piece of A4 and put it up at the entrance: CLOSED TILL FURTHER NOTICE.

I slept all day, and spent the night sitting in Lil's kitchen until I fell asleep with my head on the table. At some stage I was aware of someone coming in (I could tell it was Becky Sharp) and placing a shawl around my shoulders, but I didn't acknowledge her. When I woke in the morning, Kate was sitting at the table, watching me.

'I want her brought home,' she said. 'We can look after her ourselves, and prepare her for burial. Bathsheba says you *can*.'

———

And so we brought Lil home.

Covered by a sheet, she was carried through the house on a stretcher by two men. Bathsheba went before them, leading the way to Lil's room, where she flicked a protective covering over the bed and lowered the blind to half-mast. The room dimmed.

Lil's former bulk had diminished. For a moment I felt I didn't know her, with all the life gone out. Then Kate hurried across the room and bent down to kiss her on the forehead, and the cheek. She stayed there with her forehead pressed to Lil's, and suddenly she was my Lil again, home again at Samarkand for the last time.

And now, we must wash and dress her. At first I was anxious and afraid, but then I saw that after all, this was Lil, just Lil. And I mustn't cry. It was no time for tears, but for forbearance and love. I remembered her alive: her lap, which we had sat on as children, and leaning back into her bosom. Her hands, impatiently tugging knots from my hair. Her plump, dimpled thighs beneath a bath towel as she laboured down the hallway from the bath. She had once seemed apparently made from dough. Now she had withered and shrunk. The bones of her feet stood out, and the skin stretched over them was mottled and cold.

Kate and I had no experience of such things, but Bathsheba had, and under her supervision, we worked with tender, increasing confidence. We spoke little. I've always known that the body is a leaky thing. I myself am constantly prone to inopportune seepages, so it is only to be expected that after death the body continues with various dribblings which must be staunched and stopped.

But nothing about the human body disgusts or surprises me.

Together, Kate and I ritually sponged her. She was a much-loved territory, which for years had meant home for us, and covered by landmarks – scars, blotches and wrinkles. There was not one part of her that we did not tenderly observe.

Kate went to the wardrobe and chose a dress for her – the red one, of course – and we found her best underclothes, so that she would not go naked into that good night. And then Kate painted her face, kneeling next to her to apply foundation, powder and blusher. She chose the reddest lipstick, and outlined Lil's mouth, working with the intensity of an artist, moving away every so often to appraise her work. I wondered what Kate was thinking, and how she felt. Perhaps, like me, she found comfort in being with Lil one last time.

There was a coffin for her to be buried in, but for now we left her lying on her bed. I fetched Hetty and allowed her to pat Lil's face and crawl around and over her. Kate lay next to them, propped on one elbow, occasionally tweaking the folds of Lil's dress, or gently brushing back strands of her hair. Eventually Hetty fell asleep with her head on Lil's breast. I went to the window, and peered out through a gap at the side of the blind. Outside, the day was absolutely ordinary.

We celebrated her life that afternoon, on the broad grassy area in front of the house, with the closed coffin resting on a table.

As well as talking about former loves, it turned out that the rip-roaring conversations she'd had with her friends had also sometimes been about what they wanted done with them when they died. Lil had said she wanted a short gathering with a celebrant in front of Samarkand, followed by burial, and a party.

At Lil's request, there were no speeches, but Kate and I agreed to recite poetry. We both chose Yeats.

I chose 'A Prayer for My Daughter', which wasn't about old ladies or death. But it reflected the ties that bind people, and all our hopes and fears for them. I looked at Hetty as I recited. She sat on Bathsheba's lap and watched the proceedings, her palms pressed together and her mouth open, prepared to clap at any moment.

When it was her turn to recite, Kate walked to the front and stood for a long time without moving. Her downcast eyes and closed, pale face said *I deny funeral, I deny funeral,* but just when we thought we should continue without her, she lifted her face and recited the end of 'The Song of Wandering Aengus', in a strong, clear voice:

> *Though I am old with wandering*
> *Through hollow lands and hilly lands,*
> *I will find out where she has gone,*
> *And kiss her lips and take her hands;*
> *And walk among long dappled grass,*
> *And pluck till time and times are done*
> *The silver apples of the moon,*
> *The golden apples of the sun.*

At the cemetery she knelt, staring down into the grave when almost everyone else had departed, with an expression of absolute loss on her face, but no tears. I had to take her by the arm and lift her to her feet and walk her away.

———

It wasn't until the day after the funeral that Kate and I started sorting through Lil's things. Bathsheba and Mavis had offered to do it, but this was something Kate and I needed to do ourselves.

170

That wardrobe full of dresses! I pulled them out and stuffed them into garbage bags. The same with what Lil called her 'smalls' (though they were rather large, those underpants like bloomers – she'd been a stout old thing). Then all her make-up. 'I'll keep that,' said Kate, tipping it unceremoniously into a box.

The personal things! Letters, postcards, odds and ends. We decided on a bonfire later.

Then there were her son Alan's things, which Lil must have kept ever since his death. His suit, which Kate had worn to the school formal only a year ago. 'I don't want to throw it out,' Kate said. 'Lil never did.'

She took it for herself, though I doubted she'd ever wear it again.

While Kate was out at the loo, I went through a box of Alan's stuff, obviously sent back home after his death. His passport was there, and a pile of small notebooks, all labelled *Ideas for Stories.* I looked inside, and saw that they'd been mostly written in shorthand. On one of the flyleaves, something was written in a child's bold handwriting. I remembered writing it.

I didn't have time to read the notebooks now, so I set them aside for later.

I also found an old Polaroid photo of Alan, with a girl. The colour was so washed out they looked like ghosts. I knew that I should show it to Kate. When she came back, I handed it to her without saying anything, and she said after a while, 'She looks a lot like you.'

Looking up at me, she said, 'It's *her*, isn't it?' When I didn't reply, she slipped it into the pocket of her shirt.

———

It was past midnight by the time we'd finished sorting Lil's things.

'What now?' said Kate.

I grabbed the two bags of dresses, and carried them out. She followed me. 'Sophie! *Say* something to me!'

I hauled them down the steps and along the dark street, with Kate running behind. The metal walkway of the bridge gleamed under the streetlights as I made my way across. In the middle of the bridge I set down the bags. I looked right, to the dark shape of Planet Music and left to the Winsome Hotel (some soul possibly still awake in a single lit-up room on the top floor), and then down into the water. I ripped open the bag and started throwing the clothes over the side.

'Sophie, don't!' Kate tried to grab hold of each dress as I pulled it out like a rabbit from a hat, but I was too quick for her. Over the side it went, and floated like a shadow on the water.

'Sophie!'

Kate's taller than I am, and she tried to physically restrain me, but like a lunatic I kept breaking free and dancing beyond her grasp. 'You *always* throw stuff into the river when you want not to be reminded of things!' she said. 'And I *won't* have you throwing Lil away!'

I stopped. 'Do I? Throw stuff in the river when I don't want to be reminded?'

'Yes, you know you do.'

I hadn't known she'd noticed me do that. But my blood was wild and hot, and I felt compelled to toss away the dresses until the bags were empty. The water below the bridge was littered with frocks, some billowing, some waterlogged and beginning to sink. I tore open the second bag.

Kate whipped the Polaroid out of her top pocket and held it aloft. 'If you keep on, I'll rip this up and throw it in as well!'

Two pedestrians excused themselves, and edged past us, hands in pockets.

'You wouldn't.'

'You don't know me.'

I looked into her eyes. She was right. I didn't know her.

'Give it to me.'

'No. Stop, or I'll tear it up!' she said excitedly. And without more ado, she ripped the picture in two – just like that – and let it drop into the river.

We both looked down into the water, but it was so dark and the picture so small it wasn't visible.

Kate's lip began to quiver, and she stepped forward and pounded me on the chest, with her clenched fist, four times. I counted.

'So!' she said.

'So.'

She heaved a sigh.

'Look,' I said. By that stage I was calm through and through. It felt odd after my bout of madness. 'I'm *not* throwing Lil away. I think she'd have wanted this. What are we going to do with these dresses of hers otherwise? Keep getting them out and poring over them at intervals till we're old ladies? Give them to an op shop? Do you really want to walk down the street and see old women, or worse, girls *our* age, kitted out in these? They're awfully old and musty and desirable.'

Kate pulled Lil's ancient op-art shift from the bag and put it to her nose.

'It smells of her,' she whispered, a tear running down her face.

'I know.'

She regarded it for ages, and then put it up to her mouth and kissed it, and dropped it over the side of the bridge.

We took it in turns to ceremoniously remove each dress from the bag, shake it out and admire it, then close our eyes and put it to our faces briefly, before tossing it away. It became a graceful balletic dance, as each dress flew out over the side of the bridge and seemingly paused for a moment like a dancer in a spotlight, before descending into the water.

Kate got the last turn, and I could see that she couldn't let the dress go. 'We can keep just one,' she said pleadingly.

'Yes. It's a pity it's such an ugly one.' It was the silver sheath Lil used to wear to weddings and funerals, all glittery with real metal thread like chain mail.

It went the way of the others.

Thus unburdened, we picked up the empty plastic bags and walked over the bridge in the direction of the Winsome, to go the long way home.

CHAPTER THREE

LIL'S SON ALAN only ever visited us once. Lil said he'd travelled from Overseas (such an important place: it needed a capital letter even as you spoke of it). He'd come to see her and to go to a wedding, and Kate and I went with them (dressed in new identical dresses, except that Kate's was green and mine rose-pink). We stayed overnight in a family room at a motel.

Lil clearly adored him. Well, he was her child, so I understand that fully now. I remember how excited she was the day he arrived home, and not long after, how grief-stricken at the news of his death. I thought that she might never come back to us at all. Even the presence of Kate could not appease her sorrow.

I remember him as tall and brown-bearded and serious. When we were small, Kate and I shared the room that was to become mine. He came in as Lil was putting us to bed one night and said cheerfully, 'This was my room once. It's the best room in the house. Up high, with the view out the front of the river.' He stood at the doorway and looked out; it was a dark, warm night, and I can't imagine he could have seen anything much. But the expression on his face told me that he was seeing something that the rest of us couldn't.

One day, I stood at the crack of the open kitchen door and spied, as he and Lil spoke about us. 'Who *are* these children?' he said.

'I told you in my letter. They were left. I took them in. That's all there is to it.'

'But who left them?'

'Just a man. Michael O'Farrell, his name was.'

'And what else did he leave?'

'A few clothes. Their birth certificates. That's all.'

Lil rummaged in a drawer and drew something out. He looked at the pieces of paper and shook his head.

'What is it? What?'

'Nothing. You could have found him … and what about their mother?'

'He never mentioned her. I gathered she was out of the picture. Anyway, they're better off with me … is that you, Sophie? Come in if you're coming in. No good will come of listening at doorways, madam!'

———

Alan gave us a pile of books he'd bought down at the local bookshop, handing them over casually. 'Since you like stories,' he said, and not in a superior way either, as some people do, thinking them childish things. I knew that he liked stories too. He'd even told me he wrote them.

That was the day he took us to the park where he pushed us on the swings and then lay back on his elbows, long legs crossed, as Kate played in the sand with her toy cars. I stretched out beside him, feeling very grown-up. He had a notebook with him, and had been writing in it. He closed it up when he saw that I wanted to talk. He clearly enjoyed talking with us; that was one of the things I liked about him. He treated us as real, serious people.

176

First, I asked him why he was going away again, because he'd told me he was only there for a few more days.

'For adventure,' he said. 'And to find things to write about. That's how I make my living. I'm a writer. I report back to newspapers.'

'What sort of things? Can't you make it all up from here?'

'I write about real things … wars. And disasters. There's always something dreadful happening somewhere. You need to be there.'

'Isn't this real here? Can't you write about this?'

'I used to think so,' he said.

'I'm a writer,' I said, confidently.

'Are you? What do you write?'

'I can write stories! Real ones.'

He handed over his notebook. 'Write me a story, then.'

I looked at the scribble he'd been making and said, 'I write properly, not like you.'

I turned to the flyleaf and wrote a proper story with proper letters. There it was in the notebook I discovered after Lil died. It was a very simple story, only three sentences long. It was the story of my life.

My name is Sophie. I am seven years old. My mother is dead.

After we came back from leaving the dog with my grandfather, my mother's illness got worse. Once, she had walked about so smoothly and gracefully, her skirt swishing with life and determination. Now she navigated her way round the flat using the walls. I once found her in the middle of the night crawling down the hallway on her hands and knees. She found her way to bed and I covered up her legs and watched over her till I fell asleep beside her. She was very ill, I can see that now, and the child me knew it as well.

I used to comb her hair while she lay in bed, and learned to make cups of tea, which she could never finish. They went cold next to the bed. I amused Kate in front of the television, and spread bread with peanut butter for us both to eat. At least she was there with us. It was a kind of happiness, those days with her.

Her friend Loretta used to come and take us out while she stayed in bed, but I was filled with anxiety every moment I was away from her. One day when Loretta brought us back, I remember her saying to our mother ... *weak as a kitten*, but our mother insisted that she was *just tired, that's all*.

That day the ambulance came and took her away. Later, Loretta took us to the hospital, but they didn't allow us to stay very long. I can remember holding her hand. 'Be my big girl, and look after Kate,' she said. I put my fingers to her mouth and she kissed each one of them in turn, and then the same for Kate, who giggled with delight.

When we were leaving I looked back, and she was still watching us.

———

Michael O'Farrell returned. Every day he left us on our own while he went out, sometimes not arriving home till we had put ourselves to bed. I kept on asking to see our mother, but he shook his head and opened another beer. Once he found out that Loretta had taken us up to her place for the day while he was out, and he hit the roof. We were frightened to go again. I hushed Kate, and refused to answer whenever she knocked and called out.

One day he came home with a feed of fish and chips for us and told us that our mother had had to go away.

Soon after that he brought us here to Samarkand, and left us here with Lil.

———

At the old stuccoed block of flats, the sky was always a deep, unmoving blue. In the back yard there was only concrete underfoot, and a group of rotary clotheslines standing like a flock of queer birds. Her belly big with Kate, my mother would hang out the washing, telling stories all the while, so that for me all stories have an aura of sky-blue. In my mind they were just one big story anyway. The tales of children finding a gingerbread cottage in the woods or princesses dancing their shoes to pieces were associated with all the stories my mother told about how I'd been born.

'I was happy the whole time I was having you ...'

'This is the dress I wore then – I love the colours; can't bear to throw it away, but look how faded it's become.'

'There were two sisters, and one had hair as black as coal; the other's hair was as yellow as sunshine ...'

'You came into the world with your eyes wide open ...'

Once, before Kate, before Michael O'Farrell, I was a naked child on an early morning beach watching my mother go out into the waves. She submerged and came up time and again, wiping the hair from her eyes. She looked back at me and moved her arm in a great celebratory arc.

I stood at the edge and watched, my toes clamped into wet sand. I roared (before I had words I had such a strong voice!) because I had been abandoned. But my mother seemed oblivious to me, and kept walking out into the terrifying unknown waves.

Finally she halted, and began to wait for each swell to come to her, diving under each one with pure pleasure, sometimes looking back at me with a reluctant expression of anxiety and longing. When I became a mother myself, I knew that look. It's the look of a woman torn between the delight of doing what she wants and the duty of returning to her child.

Finally, my mother submerged herself one last time and returned, oh so slowly, water streaming from her long hair, over her breasts and belly and thighs.

Until she was graspable, and I possessed her again.

CHAPTER FOUR

KATE AND I WALKED away from the bridge, and each of us was lost in her own thoughts, and what hers were I couldn't imagine. She had been right in what she said before she ripped up that photo and threw it into the river. I didn't know her.

I looked sideways at her profile, her nose straight and fine, regal almost, her skin so pale that she appeared to have an inner light that spoke of a new certainty and self-possession. I wondered when she had stopped being my own darling Kate, when it was that I'd begun to move imperceptibly away from her. I think it must have been when we arrived at Samarkand and I could safely leave her in the care of Lil.

Though in truth, it was she who'd also been moving away from me. With her new-found friends and life in the city, her mobile phone and her new hair-style and confidence, she had grown up and away almost without me noticing.

'I was planning to go away after Christmas,' she said, with only a faint air of embarrassment. 'To see Alex in Europe. I've been saving all year – it won't cost much more than the fare because I'll have somewhere to stay. You don't mind, do you?'

'Why should I mind?'

'Well, I hadn't told Lil or anyone yet, and now that she's dead … I was planning to have Christmas with you all, you see. I still will.'

'I wish I was as adventurous as you.'

'Do you really? I always thought you were more adventurous. The way you just went ahead and had Hetty. I wouldn't have been so brave. I think having a child must be the biggest adventure of all.'

'I don't know about brave …'

Then she said in a rush, as though afraid of not ever saying it, 'She died, didn't she?'

'Yes.'

'I always knew that. But when your father tells you she had to go away, you kind of believe it, don't you? He seemed to have so much authority. And I was so young, I didn't really understand what anything meant at all. And then later on, you described her leaving, in her red dress and all.'

'I made it up. Poetic licence.'

'Then tell me what really happened.'

We had reached the horse that lived in the school's paddock, and stopped to pat it.

'It's a long story,' I said. 'I'll write it for you,' I said impulsively.

'Do you promise?'

'I promise. I'll begin this summer.'

———

We reached Samarkand, which stood almost in darkness, except for my room, where Becky waited for me with Hetty. It was a huge dark pile of a house, so ancient and weathered it was a wonder that anyone could ever love it.

'Do you think that *was* her with Alan in that photo?' Kate said.

'We'll probably never know.'

Kate bowed her head and did not speak. Then, looking up at Samarkand towering above us, she said, 'I love this place. It's home. Let's not ever sell it.'

'Of course not.' I reached out and straightened her collar. She smoothed the wild hair away from my face.

'We'll do,' she said, with certainty.

She put out her hand and I took it, and we walked up the stairs that way, just as we had when we were children.

CHAPTER FIVE

AND SO HERE I am in my red-room, galloping towards the end of my story. I can feel all the loose ends yearning to be gathered together; or more truthfully, I can feel you, my Dear Reader, wanting them gathered, because that is what novels are meant to do. But what if stories didn't end? What if they finished – ploof! – like that, simply because the writer got tired of writing, and wandered away?

Though I can feel myself *not* wanting to stop, because writing has become so much part of my life. I have burned a multitude of candles down to their stubs, a veritable host of long, white candles blazing away in your honour (though sometimes sputtering in a draft, and almost extinguished, because writing is a windy and uncertain business). Candle upon candle, blown out each night and relit the next.

Night follows night in the world of the novelist, who has only a candle and a computer screen and her own persistence to light the way. And that is why I say with confidence that the night belongs to us.

———

I would like to think that our lives are not mere chance. That there is a pattern and meaning to them (and isn't that what novels are about? So why not our lives?). I like to think that, before she died, our mother told Michael O'Farrell to bring us to Lil.

Before Alan went away, he drew me towards him and kissed the top of my head. 'I'll send postcards,' he promised.

He was killed before he sent even one. But he did give me something after all because now, among Lil's things, I've discovered his notebooks written in shorthand. In one, he has recorded a conversation with a girl. It goes something like this. No – I have the notebook here. It goes exactly like this:

'I'm not going to get dressed yet. I'm going to lie here naked, and bask. You know, what I like about sex is that it's essentially ridiculous.'

'You think so?'

'Don't you? God, this room is – such – an – awful – colour! It ought to be red.'

'Why?'

'Just because ... What's that book you're writing in?'

'It's a secret scribbled notebook.'

'Mysterious! And? *What* are you writing?'

'I'm putting down everything we say. Hurry up and get dressed; my mother will be home soon.'

'What's she like?'

'She's lovely. She has a heart of gold. And she's as mad as a hatter.'

'I like the sound of her ... Anyway, what will you do with all this stuff you're scribbling down?'

'Don't know. I could write a story.'

'About ... ?'

'A girl too beautiful for her own good, and too restless.'

'Are only men allowed to be restless? I could come with you, to Asia ... anyway, I'm getting out of home as soon as I can.

I want to go somewhere! I *hate* living on that wet old mountainside with my father. Okay! I'm getting dressed as fast as I can! What did I do with my shoes?'

———

And in my imagination, my mother looks over her shoulder at him as she bends down and slips a blue, embroidered Chinese slipper onto her foot. And inside her body a single sperm reaches its target, and a zygote is formed.

But that's far too romantic! Why shouldn't the conception happen while she coughs, or sneezes, or farts? This is a modern novel after all, and one after my own, curious, wayward heart.

She farts. 'Sorry!' she says automatically, though what's a small fart between friends, or lovers?

He puts his arms around her.

And just once, for one single moment, I am the third that lies in their embrace.

———

And now here I am in the red-room, having come full circle, my odyssey completed. I am home.

This morning when I woke, Becky was still sleeping. She had her arms thrown above her head. Hetty lay between us; she usually ends up in our bed. At moments like that I want time to stand still. I want to keep them both here with me, the way I once wanted to keep my mother, with my hands forever tangled in her hair.

But you can't capture anything. Everything changes. And as a way of preserving, even writing seems futile.

Sometimes I find myself wanting to extract from Becky Sharp that ultimate lovers' promise: that she will love me for ever and ever.

But I won't ask that, because *ever and ever* is impossible. I know that all any of us ever has is now.